Also by VALERIE HOBBS

SONNY'S WAR

SONNY'S WAR

VALERIE HOBBS

FRANCES FOSTER BOOKS • FARRAR, STRAUS AND GIROUX
NEW YORK

Library of Congress Cataloging-in-Publication Data

Hobbs, Valerie.

Sonny's war / Valerie Hobbs.— 1st ed.

p.   cm.

Summary: In the late 1960s, fourteen-year-old Cory's life is greatly changed by the sudden death of her father and her brother's tour of duty in Vietnam.

ISBN 0-374-37136-9

1. Vietnamese Conflict, 1961–1975—United States—Juvenile fiction.   2. United States—History—1961–1969—Juvenile fiction.   [1. Vietnamese Conflict, 1961–1975—United States—Fiction.   2. United States—History—1961–1969—Fiction.   3. Brothers and sisters—Fiction.   4. Death—Fiction.]   I. Title.

PZ7.H65237 So 2002
[Fic]—dc21

2002023891

FOR MY MOM

ACKNOWLEDGMENTS

My heartfelt appreciation goes once again to
Frances and to the members of my amazing writing group:
Ellen, Hope, Judy, Mary, Mary 2, Lee, Lisa, and Marni.

SONNY'S WAR

1

AFTER DAD DIED, I couldn't let loose of Sonny. I'd follow him everywhere, even out to the garage to watch him work
on the Ford, handing him stuff he needed. At first I didn't
know a lug nut from a walnut, so I wasn't much use. But after a
while, I'd know what to get before Sonny even asked.

I was fourteen, a girl full of questions, the hard-to-answer
kind. But Sonny let me blab all I wanted, even about the dumb
stuff, like boys and school. He didn't say much, but he listened
the way only Sonny listened, with his whole self. He'd tell me
not to sweat it, whatever it was. And then we'd laugh, kind of,
because that's what Dad always said.

I loved Sonny with horse blinders on. Even if he didn't have
a lot of friends, nobody was as smart or good-looking or as
brave as my brother. He was my lighthouse, my path through
the woods, my best friend.

He believed in me, even when he didn't believe in himself.

It was summer and the devil winds were back, blowing in

over the mountains like they surely meant us harm. Sonny had been working on the Ford since morning, straight through the hottest part of the day, we couldn't understand how. All Mom and I could do was fan our faces with the lunch menus and argue. About what would happen to the restaurant, about Sonny and his car, and then about Dad.

I hated the way she just accepted whatever the doctors told her. To me, a father couldn't go into a hospital with a bad cold and come out dead of a heart attack unless some pretty big mistakes got made. Mom was crying, and the more she cried the meaner I got.

Feckless started whining at the door. Sure as anything, as soon as she got outside, she'd be scratching to get back in. In and out, in and out. She'd give us those sad brown eyes, but we couldn't tell her the truth. No matter where she looked, she just wasn't going to find Dad.

Mom got up to open the door, and there was Sonny, covered with grease, a wrench loose in his hand. Mom let out a yelp before she saw that it was him. It was as if he'd grown two feet overnight, stretched out skinny like saltwater taffy, and his voice sounded like somebody else was coming out of there, a full-grown man.

"Got 'er runnin'," he said. You had to see his eyes. Sonny's eyes always said what he couldn't stick together with words.

"That's fine, son," Mom said in her ghost voice. Most of the time since Dad died she was someplace else, which was where her voice came from. We all sounded different, and I guess we *were* different. Three learning how not to be four.

I got up and followed Sonny. Outside, I grabbed my throat and screamed like I was being strangled. Sonny didn't even flinch. He was already used to the way Mom and I were being.

The garage smelled of grease and cigarettes. Sonny didn't smoke then, but the other guys always did. They'd smoke until there was nothing left to pinch. Then they'd smash the butts on the floor. Sometimes you could hardly see the guys in there for all that smoke.

The Ford's hood was open, and there were patches of clean fender where the guys had leaned in. The engine was shiny and new-looking, the way the car would never look on the outside. It needed a paint job bad.

Sonny closed the hood the way you do when you really love a car, catching it halfway, pressing it down easy with his palm. A streak of grease cut into his long, dark hair where the sun had bleached it out a little. I thought about how grownup and handsome he was, even with his broken nose that never got right, and his greasy jeans sagging like old man's pants.

"Listen, Cory," he said, as if we shared a special secret, and slid into the driver's seat. He turned the key and that big engine came alive.

"Hop in!" he said, his grin a quick flash.

Backing out the driveway, he swung onto Ojala Avenue, left arm riding the ledge of the open window. He was hoping the guys would be at the Frostee or the Esso station where he worked, I knew without his saying, but it was early. Passing Saint Thomas Aquinas church, I thought about how he'd get a girl for sure now that he had the car running, and that she would snuggle right up next to him, not over by the door, shotgun, where I was.

He'd have to work fast though, unless he just wasn't going to Vietnam.

We rode without talking, out toward the mountains on the north end of town. The sky was bluing to black, and a few stars had popped out. Real romantic, I guess, if you weren't brother and sister.

"I'm gonna leave the keys with you, Sis," Sonny said after a while. "You can start her once a week so she doesn't freeze up. Give her a wash now and then if you want to."

I could tell he'd been thinking about how he was going to say all that, so there was this lump in my throat I couldn't talk over. Then I said he didn't have to worry, that I'd take good care of all of his stuff. I started to cry, all snot-nosed and sniffling. Just when the air would dry some tears up, more would come. Sonny kept glancing over, worried. After a while he pulled off the road, cut the engine, and sat fiddling with his keys.

"Shitcakes," I said. It was a word I saved for special occasions, but it didn't help. In light of the way things were, our father dead and the war hanging over us, words didn't matter much. Not unless the President said them, or you read your name on a draft notice.

We sat there on the side of the road, listening to the cicadas singing to the crickets, and then them singing back. We didn't know how to say things in our family, never did. Not even after the funeral when it was just the three of us back at the restaurant, sitting at a four-top like we were waiting for the check.

"You going for sure?" I said.

"Yup." In the glow of the dash, Sonny's knuckles showed all their scrapes and nicks. The grease wasn't ever coming out of those fingernails, even the Army couldn't do that. "It's that or jail."

"But you could get out. You know, because of Dad."

"Yeah, I heard that."

"The Army would let you out."

"Yeah."

"Then why are you going?"

Sonny shrugged. He wouldn't look at me. He just wanted out of there, out of our nowhere little town, and this was a way.

"Crap," I said.

"You've got a real bad mouth for a girl, Cory." He started the engine and wheeled the Ford around fast, so that we were heading back the way we came.

"I'll show you how she goes," he said, which is how I knew he wasn't really mad.

If you've ever been to Ojala, you know there's only one road coming in, and it's the same road that goes out. All around are the mountains, a ring of peaks so high they get snow. When we came to California the year before, when I was hating it with

7

every breath, I said Ojala was like a trap. I thought I was being clever, but it was the truth. Kids like us, the kind without money, could get stuck there forever and think it was a life.

The sign for 101 North rose up out of the dark. Sonny punched the gas and the speedometer climbed, 65, 70, 75. Something inside me fuzzed over and settled. From the first, I loved speed, and so did Sonny.

"So what do you think?" He held her loose, but I knew he could handle her. He lived for cars and not much else. Now that he had the Ford running, he could race her at the drags. You had to do that to get listened to in the crowd he ran with, Jason and the others, but especially Jason.

"She sounds great," I yelled, as we shot straight through the night, the blotted shapes of trees and split-rail fences, a house now and then, passing fast as flip cards. The dark inside the car made a peaceful space we couldn't find at home.

In a flash, the peaceful dark was gone. Light washed over Sonny's face. He glanced into the rearview mirror, surprised. Somebody was behind us and coming on fast.

"Who is it?" Sonny peered into the mirror. "I can't tell."

Squinting, I could see only the fuzzy dark outline of two heads behind the high beams. "Nobody," I said. "Not the cops though." But the car kept on our bumper, close, like the two guys inside knew us, cats after mice. Then Sonny put his foot in it and the Ford jumped ahead, leaving the strangers behind.

"Sweet," I said, because that's how it felt, that big souped-up engine carrying us away, and nobody anywhere, just the dark and the few stars.

Then they were back in the mirror again, their headlights growing fast. "I'll bet it's Jason," said Sonny, his voice gone up a notch. If it was Jason, there would be a race to the end, where the freeway petered out into Oak View.

Sonny worked his jaw the way he did when he was worried or scared. But it wasn't Jason. It wasn't anybody we knew. They were men, old men at least forty, in a red-and-white Impala, brand-new. The passenger window came down and a hand popped out waving a bottle of beer. The dark cave of a mouth yelled something that got ripped away by the wind. We were going 80, them and us, fender to fender. Then Sonny mashed the pedal, leaving the Chevy behind as if it were parked. But it came on again.

"There must be something extra under that hood," Sonny said, his hands gripping the wheel. "It sure isn't stock." I could see the Adam's apple ticking away in his throat.

The Ford was winding out like it had been waiting for just this time, 85, 90, 100. "Slow down, Sonny," I yelled, no longer brave and not caring if he knew it. But I could see he was way beyond hearing, his eyes wide and fixed ahead at some point, maybe a pinpoint, in the dark where we would break through and things would be right again.

And then it was all sirens and red lights, everywhere at once like a movie. Sonny leaned forward. He looked left and right, as if there might be an out. Then he let the engine down the way you put a baby to bed, with all that tenderness.

The cops weren't real bad guys in Ojala, you had to give them that. Some were big brothers of guys we knew, some were just kids themselves, but Ojala being a western town, they had to play it out right, spread-eagling Sonny against the cruiser, before they put him in. Sonny didn't say a word, not one, not even when they put the handcuffs on.

I cussed them out and they made me ride in the back of Sonny's car while some rookie drove. Sal Garcia's big brother, riding shotgun, told me he'd tape my mouth if I didn't shut up. They wouldn't say why they let the Impala go.

Jail was more like a bedroom than a cell, but the bars were real all right. It gave me the creeps to see my brother in a place like that, even for one week. "Reckless driving" they called it. Sonny was lucky his sentence wasn't longer. But they'd let him out for lunch and I'd take him a bologna sandwich to eat in the park. Then he'd go back to his cell and read car magazines. It was a small town, after all. They knew Sonny wasn't going anywhere.

At night, Mom and I watched the war on TV. If you didn't have a brother just the right age, you could watch it like it wasn't real, body bags being loaded into the back hatch of an airplane. Walter Cronkite would tell us how it was going, what the body count was, where President Johnson was dropping the bombs, and make it all seem no more than a thing that was happening, over there, to somebody else.

"Maybe they won't take him now," Mom said one night, "now that he's a criminal."

"He's *not* a criminal," I said.

"Well, he's a jailbird." She made a sour face.

"We could go to Canada," I said.

"We could," she said. It was an old idea, mostly mine. Whenever Canada came up, Mom would speak for Dad, who wasn't around to say his piece. "Sonny should do his duty," she'd say, but the words didn't fit her the way they did Dad, and after a while she stopped saying them.

"Sonny's gonna go," I said one night out of the blue. "He wants to go."

Mom got up, flipped off the TV, and went downstairs. "I don't know what to think anymore. I can't stand any of it," she said.

I sat staring at the gray eye of the screen, thinking that if it was me getting drafted, well, maybe I'd go, too.

Mom had visited Sonny only on the first day. After that she couldn't bring herself to go. "Mortified," she said. That was how it felt to be the mother of a jailbird. So I went by myself the day he got out.

He was standing in front of the station with the Chief, holding the blue duffel bag Dad had given him for Christmas and a potted plant. The Chief said the plant was for Mom. The three of us walked around the back to where the Ford was waiting, covered with dust. "Lighten up with that foot," the Chief said, and patted Sonny on the back.

"Heck," Sonny said, a block from the Frostee, "let's just go home." But he didn't turn off.

The Frostee was jammed. Cars everywhere, and people all over the cars. Jason's black Deuce was parked first in the driveway facing the street, and Jason himself with a Coors in his hand leaned against the driver's door. Everybody else fanned out from there, like moths in the glare of the Frostee sign, and I saw Jason turn, and then everyone else as we pulled in, the Ford purring, light bouncing off what was left of the paint. Jason raised his fist and punched the air in a victory sign, and everybody started yelling and cheering. You should have seen Sonny's face when he knew it was all for him.

2

HOW A CAR can change a life is something we all knew, so it was no surprise how the kids came around, how Sonny became Somebody almost overnight. The Ford was number six, then four, then finally the one right behind Jason, Numero Uno, in the driveway of the Frostee. Jason would throw an arm around Sonny's shoulders like they'd been best friends forever. He made it look like he wasn't worried about losing out to Sonny. And, anyway, Sonny didn't have that much time left.

Goose Henderson and Luis Moreno were going, too, drafted just like Sonny. The three of them were heroes now, kids who were invisible before. A month left and they talked about going to the war as if it weren't really them.

"Heard about this guy who stopped eating, I mean *stopped*," Goose said one night when we were cruising. "Got so skinny he looked like paper."

"They sent him home?" Luis was one of the happiest kids we knew, stone blind to the dark side of things. When he talked, he bounced on the backseat like a ten-year-old. I had to sit next to him because Goose always got shotgun.

"Sure, what do you think?" Goose had all the answers. "You can get braces put on your teeth. That'll get you out." He knocked Sonny on the shoulder. "Hey, your old man's dead, right?"

Sonny turned, a look in his eyes that would have warned a smarter person.

"Well, hey, man! That could get you out. Your mother being a widow and all."

Sonny just stared ahead at the road.

"Party time!" Goose yelled, craning that long white neck out the window. There was just the Avenue to cruise, down to the bowling alley, back up to the turnaround tree, so you saw the same people over and over. "Party time!"

I only got to cruise twice, then Sonny dropped me off at the restaurant. It was dark, except for the one light upstairs where Mom and Feckless were. Feckless had shown up one morning when Dad was peeling potatoes and she wouldn't go away. Wherever Dad went, there Feckless would be. Now she was following Sonny around. She'd whine whenever Sonny left her home and pace the floor until he returned. Nothing was the same anymore, and she didn't know what to do about it.

She wasn't the only one.

Our father was a drunk. There are nicer ways to say it, and Mom said them all, but that was the truth. Always he made it look like he was just drinking a beer, one lousy beer, but there'd be another bottle around somewhere. Mom would find the empty bottles in the trash. He'd stuff them way down, but she'd find them anyway. He didn't mind when she emptied his beer down the drain. "Aw, Evie," he'd say, "a guy's gotta have his beer." He'd sing hymns and stir the spaghetti sauce, weaving on his feet.

You had to admire the way they did it, our parents. They came all the way from Portland (Oregon, not Maine, but still . . .), and started a business practically from scratch. The house they rented had once been some kind of Welsh restaurant, and it needed lots of work. But it was right on the Avenue, which pleased Dad, and it had a big old-fashioned porch for Mom to fall in love with. I thought the place was a terrible mess and said so, but nobody was listening to me, not even Sonny that time. He'd gone right out and found his job at the Esso.

In less than three months, Mom and Dad had the place looking great. OJALA CAFÉ, EST. 1966 said the sign in blue-and-gold swirls, hanging by chains over the porch steps.

We lived upstairs under the eaves, our rooms separated by sheets, listening to the creaky pipes that never shut up. Mom said it was temporary. First we had to get on our feet. We lived like rats in the attic, I said, we had to get on our claws. She didn't like that much.

Dad started getting sick in January, when the cold settled in and you forgot you lived in California. It started with a cough, nothing more than that, but the cough wouldn't go away. It was the cigarettes, Dad said, so he cut down from two packs to one. One cigarette burning the edge of the prep table, instead of one there and another one somewhere else.

If you know cooks, you know that's how it is.

They put him in the hospital for tests. Three days, Dr. Loomis said, three days and he'd be home again, good as new. For him, it was a vacation, a nice quiet place where he could get waited on, even if the food wasn't fit for human consumption. He flirted with the oldest nurse, the grouchy one, until he got a smile out of her. Then he got a cigarette, and then he got the pack they took away in the first place.

The first day, Mom and Sonny and I were scared as anything. But Dad made us laugh at his same old jokes. So the second day we brought a picnic lunch—cold roast lamb on Dad's famous rolls, poppy-seed coleslaw, Mom's rhubarb pie. "What, no beer?" Dad said.

On the third day, a nurse caught Sonny with Feckless under his jacket and kicked them both out. Sonny went around to the window where Dad could wave to them. That was the last time any of us saw Dad.

Mom said that was the problem with Sonny.

"What problem?" I said.

"Shock," she said. "Sonny's in shock. That's why he's so quiet."

———

Nobody planned the bon voyage party for the guys. It just sort of happened in the empty lot across from Saint Thomas

Aquinas. Jimbo brought the orange crates and doused them with gasoline, and that was the signal. Cars started coming from all directions, engines rumbling, circling like big cats. After a while, the cops would clear us out, but that only made things happen faster.

Sonny said since it was a special night, I could stay for one hour. But if I took so much as one sip of beer, I was dead.

I kept my mouth shut, which was hard, and counted cars. I was up to sixteen when Jason came idling across the lot. Nose to the fire, his black Deuce seemed to go straight up in flames. He got out and closed his door. Leaning against the hood of the Deuce, he crossed his arms to make the muscles pop out. August heat and the fire besides, but Jason looked cool as a Popsicle. Jimbo fetched him a beer without asking. Sheila, his sometime girlfriend, pushed in under his arm.

"Hey, Sonny. Goose. Hey, Luis," Jason said.

"Hey, Jason." Together, like a chorus.

Jason had a wicked grin. There was too much in it besides what you saw. "You and me. Right, Sonny?"

Sonny didn't get it, not at first.

"Carne Road. You and me."

"You can't, Sonny—" It was out of my mouth like a wound-up canary.

"Hush, Cory," Sonny said, no more than a whisper.

I should have known from the way the Ford had moved up in the Frostee line, one week back with the nobodies and then right up there behind Jason. I should have known this would happen.

"I'm not racing her on the street," Sonny said.

"Carne Road," Jason said with a huge shrug, as if that made sense, as if a road wasn't a street. "We'll have lookouts for the cops," Jason said with mean little eyes. "You owe me."

Sonny didn't ask why. He knew there wasn't a reason. It was just the stupid way Jason saw things.

We watched Jason head off toward the beer keg.

"You can't, Sonny. You're on proba—" My words got smothered in the crowd, kids who'd picked up the scent of a hunt, and now homed in around Sonny.

"You can dust that Deuce!"

"You're not a chicken, are you, Sonny?"

"Hey, everybody! Sonny and Jason are going to race! Midnight! Carne Road."

3

DAD DIED ON THE THIRD DAY. He had an "episode," Dr. Loomis said. The episode had stuck in his heart and killed him.

Right then, I could tell how little that doctor really knew.

Sonny told Mom he'd take care of the "funeral stuff." That's how Sonny said it, because that's all we really knew about what happened after. You could tell that it hadn't sunk in for Mom yet that Dad was gone. She would wander around the darkened restaurant from room to room as if she expected him to pop out of hiding. He wasn't above doing a thing like that, playing some nutty trick. You never knew when he'd stick his finger up his nose and pull out a straw wrapper squeezed like an accordion, or do an Irish jig.

When Sonny told Mom we'd go to Baggets' and arrange things, she just nodded. Yes, that was the best thing to do, she said, as if Sonny was so smart to have thought about a funeral. Her eyes cleared for just two seconds, and then they got misty. "Dad was so proud of you both," she said.

There were people around Mom those days, more people than we thought she knew. Neighbors or "regulars," like Sam the bald-headed movie man and Maria the ex-opera star. But they could only do so much. They'd hang out in the dining room, where the chairs were stacked upside down on all the tables but the one, and drink pots of coffee. Mom would wait on them, just like before, as if the Ojala Café was still open.

Sam had a crush on Mom, even Dad knew that. He was our most regular "regular" and now he was lost, just like the rest of us. Without Dad, there was no café. It was almost as if it had never been.

Baggets' was the only funeral home in town, so there wasn't a question of where we would go. Sonny and I dressed up as best we could. Sonny's suit pants were way too short and his wrists stuck out of his sleeves, but I said he looked good for a grease monkey. I wore one of Mom's frilly blouses with an itchy wool skirt I hadn't worn since Oregon. Sad as we were, it was hard not to laugh at the way we looked.

Strange how you can pass a place every day and never think about it, about what it could mean to your life. Baggets' Funeral Home was right next to the bowling alley at the far end of the Avenue. It was a yellow stucco box with squared-off hedges all around it, and the grass was always green, even in the middle of summer when everybody else had brown stubble.

You had to wonder about that.

Sonny pulled into the parking lot and turned off the ignition. At first, we didn't move. But my skirt itched so bad under-neath, I couldn't sit for long. I got out first and waited. Finally, Sonny got out, too.

"Dad wouldn't want anything fancy," he said, like he was talking to himself, and maybe he was. He scratched the back of his neck, then straightened his tie, Dad's tie, the one with the ducks.

Robert Bagget was waiting behind his big maple desk with the glass top, nothing on it but his two clean white hands. Robert was the older brother, the one who did the talking. The other one did all the dirty work, but that could have been ru-mor.

"We were so sorry to hear about your father," he said, but the way his face was, it was hard to tell if he really meant that. It was a round and happy man-in-the-moon kind of face, and I kept trying to see him upside down.

Anyway, how could he really be sorry when people died? It was how he made his money.

Papers appeared out of nowhere, like a card trick. Sonny answered all the questions, a line of sweat across his forehead and under his nose. The room was so quiet you couldn't sigh or shift much in your chair, even if your skirt itched, without it causing a commotion. I just knew if Dad were there he'd do something, like tell a joke or fart. A giggle almost got loose be-fore I swallowed it down, quick.

"Well," Robert Bagget said at last. He set the papers to one side. You could tell he was satisfied about something, but that we probably didn't have to know what that was. He stood up and we did, too. "Let's take a look at the caskets, shall we?"

I grabbed Sonny's sleeve and, for the first time since the day I wet my pants in kindergarten, Sonny let me take his hand. The soft gray carpet didn't look dangerous at first, but you kept sinking way down into it, how far was hard to guess, maybe all the way down where they did the bodies. I kept gulping for air they'd sucked out of the room along with the sound.

Robert Bagget opened a double door and out came soft organ music, the kind they played in church before the collection basket got passed around.

He stepped aside to let us go in first.

All the light in the room came from hidden places up near the ceiling, like light from the heads of angels. That way you didn't notice right away how ugly the three caskets were, cardboard boxes covered with wallpaper, one pink, one blue, one silver but the exact same otherwise. I wanted to touch one. But then again, I didn't. I wanted to know if they were really made of cardboard. I didn't think you were allowed to bury a person in cardboard.

"These are the choices for Plan A," Robert Bagget said with a tiny frown on the forehead of his moon face. "All quite . . . serviceable. I would suggest the silver one, if, of course, you decide to go with Plan A."

I wanted to ask Sonny what Plan A was, but my mouth, for

once, was stuck closed. I couldn't remember Robert Bagget saying anything about Plan A when we were in the other room.

The way he read my mind was spooky. "Plan A, as you remember, keeps you within the fifteen hundred dollar range."

Fifteen hundred dollars? I shot a look at Sonny. Maybe there was some money I didn't know about, but fifteen hundred dollars? That was a lot of money.

"Now Plan B," Robert Bagget said, moving toward another door, "gives you several other options."

In the second room, the light was brighter, even the music was happier, and all the caskets were made of wood. Sonny reached out like he was in a dream and laid his hand on a honey-colored casket with curly brass handles that shone like gold.

"A fine choice," Robert Bagget said. He cupped a hand on Sonny's shoulder. He went on about all the features of Plan B as he kind of pushed Sonny out of the room.

––––––––––

Back in the car with the doors closed, I almost exploded from waiting. "Sonny! Where are we gonna get twenty-five hundred dollars? What's Mom going to say when you tell her how much it's gonna cost? Did you know how much funerals were? Huh? And what about the service? Is that extra?"

"Calm down, Cory," Sonny said. "You saw what there was. I couldn't bury Dad in that silver thing." He started the car. "Don't worry, I'll get the money."

But I couldn't calm down. Twenty-five hundred dollars. Dad had paid that for the Dodge and it was still running fine. "Where are you going to get that much money, Sonny?"

"Don't worry, I said. I'll get it from the Army. I'll send every cent I make." By the angry sound of his voice, I could tell he was talking to somebody else. To Robert Bagget. Sonny knew he'd been taken. Even I knew that.

"I don't think you're going to make that much, Sonny."

"I couldn't bury him in that silver thing, Cory," Sonny said. There was a catch in his voice and I was afraid he might cry.

4

THE BONFIRE WAS BLAZING HIGH as the steeple at Saint Thomas Aquinas. Sonny was sipping a beer. It was all he would ever drink, just one. But it made him easy, and he let me stay past an hour. Mom knew I was with Sonny. I was always with Sonny. She would worry, but not too much. The way she and I argued, it was better than having me home.

A fire siren wailed at the other end of the Avenue. Kids started moving toward their cars, taking their time, swilling a last beer. It wasn't any use to argue. The volunteers would come and put out the fire. Maybe the cops would come, too, maybe not. Nobody got too excited about it. It was the way things had been since the fifties. The whole town was stuck in the past.

"See you at Carne Road," Jason said, sliding into his Deuce. He gave Sonny a two-fingered salute. Then he revved his big engine and drove off.

Sonny and I were the last to leave. "Let's just go home, Sonny," I said. Either way, I knew that's where I'd be going. We watched Ojala's pride-and-joy fire truck come barreling across the lot. Four volunteers jumped out and went to work. In no time our fire was just a sorry mess of smoke.

Sonny started the Ford and we idled across the lot to the Avenue. Something about the way he was driving gave him away. "You're going to do it, aren't you?"

A streetlight splashed over Sonny's face. For a minute, he didn't look like anybody I knew. He looked bleached out, his gray eyes like black stones. "Yeah. I guess."

"Take me with you! Please, please, Sonny?"

"Cory—"

"I have to. Please! I have to go with you."

He stopped at the Avenue, looked at me, shook his head, and grinned. Then he turned right.

"I won't say a word. I promise."

"That'll be the day!" Sonny laughed.

So I shut up. But the closer we came to Carne Road, the sicker I got. There were kids who had died racing on Carne Road, going straight into the rocks at the end, a twisted heap of metal and blood. They were heroes, too, only they were dead.

We needed a real police force, people said, a police force "with teeth." But nothing changed. Street racing was in the blood of the town. Even some of the cops had raced when they were in high school. Ojala was a town too lazy to change. People married straight out of high school and never left, working at jobs that somebody had to do, like checking groceries at Bayley's or teaching school. If you wanted to know what Ojalans thought, you could read the editorials in the *Ojala Sun*. That's how people made up their minds about things like putting in a streetlight and sending troops to Vietnam. Yes on both.

Past the bowling alley, the Avenue went straight and dark until it met Carne Road on a blind curve. Sonny slowed the Ford to an idle. It was so quiet, you couldn't tell anybody was there, but we knew the cars were threaded all through the orange groves, their lights and radios off. Hanging over everything in that dark sky was just a wink of moon.

"I don't care if you win," I said, as Sonny turned into the grove. "You don't have to win," I said. "Who cares anyway?" My words came out in little bursts, like a popgun. I felt like throwing up.

Sonny turned off the engine, pulled out the keys. There were just the two besides the Ford key, one for home and one for the Esso station. He spilled the keys back and forth, back and forth, watching his hands. Somebody in a nearby car hooted. Then everything was quiet again, except for the sound of those keys. "Mom said Dad was proud of us, you know? But he wasn't proud of me."

"That's not true, Sonny," I said. I sounded exactly like Mom, that same voice that didn't convince anybody.

"Hey, I'm not crying about it. I just wish he could be around for when I come back from the war, you know?" Sonny looked out the window into the shadows of the trees. "I'm going to make him proud," he said.

I was shaking in that deep place that won't let up once it starts, no matter what you do.

"Hey," Sonny said softly, looking over. "Hey, Cory. Come on, I'll take you home."

"No! I'll be all right. I promise. You can't take me—"

Jason's face popped up in the window over Sonny's left shoulder. "Hey!"

Sonny jumped.

"Ready to rumble?"

"You're on," Sonny said.

"Sissy can ride with Jimbo and them," said Jason, jerking his head toward a pair of high beams. As if on signal, engines started up all around us and lights crisscrossed through the trees where the ripe fruit hung.

Sonny started the Ford. "You okay?" he said. I nodded. I pushed open the door and got out. "Sonny?"

"Go, Sis," he said. "Go on."

I watched the taillights of the Ford bouncing away from me, Sonny taking it slow through the ruts all the way to the road.

Jimbo's pickup stopped and I climbed in the back, so crowded with kids I had to sit on Goose's lap. Goose was smashed, his head bobbing loose. I balanced myself on the end of his knees, ready to jump in case he barfed. We rocked through the trees, not the way Sonny went but all the way to the far end, where we could watch them as they came.

The wall rose up out of the dark, rocks piled so high you couldn't see the trees on the other side. Jimbo kept his motor running, his headlights on the rocks. Luis, in his father's old Merc, left his on, too.

It was quiet, kind of hushed up, as if we all recognized, for once, how small words really were. We climbed out of the pick-up, over the side or the tailgate, helping each other the way kind people do, old people, as if we all mattered. Somebody laughed, but quietly, too. Jimbo and Lisa walked arm in arm, her head on his shoulder. Goose, stumbling, tried to put his arm around me, but I shook him off. Kids piled out of Luis's father's car, too, and stood in a loose clump. A couple of kids climbed the water tower on the other side of the wall and sat on the ledge with their legs dangling.

Somebody on Luis's side said, "Jason's gonna take him," like a weather report.

I stood with my arms wrapped around my middle, shaking so hard that Lisa broke from Jimbo to put an arm around me. "Don't worry," she said, like a big sister. "Sonny's smart. Jason's an idiot, but Sonny's smart."

I couldn't see what smart had to do with it.

Jimbo heard it first and his nose went up like a retriever's. "They're coming," he said, and then I heard it, too. It was a whine at first, then a screaming wail. Four headlights grew from tiny yellow cat's eyes in the darkness. "Here they come!" Jimbo yelled, then everybody was yelling, crying out Jason's name or

Sonny's. Which was Sonny's car? How could you tell? The car on the left moved ahead, its lights the biggest, then it was the other car. Back and forth it went until, at last, they were coming straight at us, at the wall, four headlights in a line, engines pitched to howling. It was all you could hear. I felt myself crying Sonny's name, but couldn't hear it.

"God!" Goose yelled, sober. "They're not going to stop!"

Kids began backing away, sucked like a wave, farther from the wall. In the headlights, I saw Lisa's hand go up to her mouth. Jimbo looked as frightened as a horse in fire. Brakes screeched, tires squealed, and the two cars, Sonny's on the left, Jason's on the right, fishtailed to a stop, six feet from the wall. Through the smoke gone up from the tires, I saw kids run up and pull them out of their cars. Jason was laughing and so was Sonny, but you could see by their pale faces and wide eyes how close they'd come. I wanted to run up and hug Sonny for all he was worth, but he wouldn't have wanted that. I pushed through the crowd and stood next to him, close as I could get. He grinned at me and pulled me into a one-arm hug.

Jason looked over at Sonny and nodded slowly, as if he knew something now that he hadn't been sure of. "A tie," he said. "What do you know about that?"

5

MOM SPENT ALL DAY in the kitchen making Sonny his going-away dinner, studying Betty Crocker as if there was sure to be a test at the end. It was too hot to move, but for once Mom didn't notice. For a week she'd been searching for Dad's cookbook, but it had flat disappeared. I figured that would end her crazy idea to start up the café again.

"I don't understand how a big fat book can simply vanish!" she said. Dad's cookbook had been around since Day One, a faded green thing with half the pages loose. Dad wrote in the margins in handwriting that was more like hieroglyphics than English. You had to really work to read it, so nobody did.

"Come down here and taste this!" she yelled up the stairs. I was watching *The Price Is Right*, pretending it was me, or Mom, winning the new Frigidaire or the La-Z-Boy recliner.

I got up and went downstairs. Sweat made my legs stick together.

"Does it need salt?"

It was supposed to be gravy. I nodded, trying my best to swallow.

Mom frowned. "This is the third try," she said. "I used to make gravy. Didn't I? I thought I did."

I slid up on the counter to see what she'd do next.

Mom studied me for a minute, hands on her hips. Then she went to get the dust mop. "The secret to getting through the hard times is keeping busy," she said, so I pushed the mop around the dining room for a while. Then Mom came in and asked me to take down all the chairs. "I want it to look the way it did the night of the mayor's birthday. Remember? White tablecloths. A sea of napkins, folded like sailboats!" She waved her hand through the air, across the sea.

I said, "Well, we only need the one table for the three of us," but she jerked her chin like she was offended, and told me to start folding.

Sonny came in after dark smelling like Turtle Wax. Mom sent him upstairs to shower. "Dinner is just about ready," she said. She'd piled her hair on top of her head and stabbed it with a chopstick, but it wasn't holding. The white apron she'd tied three times around her waist was streaked with more colors than food ought to be. She looked beat.

"Light the candles, Cory," she said. "Please. And, for good-ness sake, comb your hair. You look like a sad sack!"

The roast beef was cooked half to death. Sonny could hardly get Dad's good knife through it, but we told Mom how great everything was, the lumpy mashed potatoes, the cold, chewy string beans.

"Here's to Sonny," Mom said, raising her glass with the two inches of sherry. Dad called it his "cooking sherry," but you never knew. We clinked glasses. The candles put a glow around our faces. Mom sipped and set her glass down. She looked at Sonny a long time and for once he didn't say, "What? What did I do?" He seemed to know she was storing him up for when he wouldn't be there.

"Don't you go being a hero, Sonny," she said. "Just do what you're told and don't volunteer for anything. Sam says that's the way to stay out of trouble."

My ears perked up. "Was Sam in the Army?" I liked Sam because he gave me free movie tickets, but I didn't like how much he was hanging around Mom, and neither did Sonny.

Mom dabbed her mouth with the white linen napkin. "He fought in Germany. He was wounded, too."

"Where?" I asked.

"I don't know. I guess in Germany."

"No, I mean where was he wounded? Like in his head, or what?"

Mom blushed bright red. "He didn't say."

"We could have thrown you a real party, Sonny," Mom said, changing the subject quick, "a going-away party. I don't know why you didn't want one."

Sonny warned me with his eyes not to say a word.

"Oh!" Mom remembered. "Grandma Davies called. She wants you to call her. And some girl—Sharon?—she called, too."

Sonny woke right up. "Sharon? Are you sure it wasn't Sheila?"

Mom thought for a minute. "Oh, well, yes. Maybe it was."

Sonny waited, his fork half up to his mouth. "Well?"

"Well, what?"

"What did she say?"

Was Sonny blushing? You couldn't really tell in that light.

"She said you could call her back if you wanted to. Her number's on the wall."

Sonny scraped his chair back.

"Not now, Sonny," Mom said, with a little sniff. "This is family time."

I couldn't wait to ask. "Who's Sheila?"

Sonny shrugged. "Just some girl."

"Jason's girlfriend? *That* Sheila?"

The front door opened and in walked four people, three men and a woman. The woman was dressed in black curtain material and a plumed hat. A droopy black feather hung over her forehead.

She flicked her eyes around the dining room at the thumb-tacked posters and all the chairs that didn't match. Then she turned to the men. "It looks like they don't get much business," she said, mouth squinched like a prune. Then out she went, the men in a line behind her.

"Oh, dear," Mom said.

Then we all started laughing. We laughed so hard even Sonny was crying.

"I suppose we should take the sign down," Mom said, wiping her eyes on a sailboat. "I figured, with Ojala, everybody just knew that when your Dad . . . when *that* happened . . ."

"I'll bet they were from L.A.," I said, a place still magical to me because of Hollywood. I'd only been there once for a field trip to the Chinese Theatre. It was only two hours away, but as different from Ojala as the moon.

Mom got up and started clearing the table. "I had a dream they sent you straight home after boot camp, Sonny. They had too many boys or something. It was the one good dream I've had since— Well."

Her mouth set, she carried Sonny's plate into the kitchen.

"I'm too stuffed for pie," she said, coming back to the table. "How about if we cruise and have our pie later."

"Cruise?" Sonny and I cried, exactly together.

"Why not?" said Mom.

That's when I knew for sure that Sonny was a grownup. He wasn't a bit embarrassed when we passed Jason on the Avenue with his car full of guys. Sonny gave the head jerk greeting, just like always, and sailed on past.

I let Mom ride shotgun, only right since it was her first and probably only time to cruise.

"So this is what you do all night?"

"This is it," Sonny said. He shrugged.

"Well, I always wondered," she said.

That wasn't all we did. Sonny was teaching me how to drive, but I wasn't legal, and she didn't have to know.

As we turned around the turnaround tree for the third time, Mom started humming softly to herself. Sonny glanced back at me, his eyebrows raised. But I knew she wasn't losing it, she was getting better her own way. Her humming and the sound of the engine made everything peaceful and safe for that little time. I felt like curling up in the seat, the way I did when I was little. I'd pretend to be sleeping so Dad would have to carry me in. All the way up the stairs he would complain about what a lug I was, then lay me down like an egg.

A siren whooped twice behind us. "Jeez!" said Sonny. "What now? I was doing twenty-five!" He pulled over to the curb and cut the engine.

Sal Garcia's brother, Mark, badge number 464, came strolling up to Sonny's window. He leaned in on his beefy hands. "Headin' out tomorrow, I heard." He was chewing Wrigley's Doublemint, you could smell it.

"That's right," Sonny said.

"Just wanted to say thank you," Mark Garcia said, offering his hand for Sonny to shake. "From me and the Chief. Well, all of us down at the station."

"Thank you?" You could tell Sonny wasn't trusting his ears.

"Goin' to defend our country, right?"

"Yes, sir."

"Eliminate the enemy. Clobber some Commies."

Sonny was grinning. You could tell he didn't know what to say. In a minute, Mark Garcia was going to have us all out of the car and marching.

"Godspeed, son," he said, clutching Sonny's shoulder. "That's all I wanted to say. Ojala is proud of its boys in uniform, you can quote me on that."

"Okay. Right! Yes, sir."

Mark Garcia whooped the siren once as he left, as a kind of farewell, I guess.

"Well, that was nice," Mom said. "Doesn't it make you feel like a part of the town?"

Sonny didn't answer, his face still caught in surprise.

Instead of going farther up the Avenue and home, Sonny turned right on Signal Street. When he made a left on Arboleda, I knew where we were headed.

It isn't much of a cemetery, but it's where you'd probably want to get buried if you thought much about it. Not a blade of grass anywhere and none of the headstones are in a straight line, but there are trees all over the place, huge old monster oaks with twisted arms and mistletoe. I guess you could see it as spooky, but I didn't.

It was dark and very quiet, but Sonny had a flashlight and we tiptoed behind him, as if we might wake somebody up.

The day we buried Dad, no one could get Sonny to leave.

The Bagget brothers were standing one on each end of the hole they'd dug, like bookends. Dad's beautiful wooden casket was on this elevator thing ready to go down, but Sonny wouldn't move. Balancing on his haunches in his too small suit, he patted and patted that shiny wooden box. It was the first time I'd seen Sonny cry like that, and he didn't even try to stop.

"Sonny, come on," I'd said. The Bagget brothers made me nervous. It was clear they weren't going anywhere, not until we did. Sonny probably signed his name to some rule in those papers that said exactly how it had to be, what did I know?

Maria, the ex-opera star, led Mom toward the Baggets' limo.

I pushed on Sonny's shoulder. "We gotta go, Sonny."

Sonny frowned up at me as if he couldn't figure out who I was. Then he slowly stood and let me pull him away.

I figured out after a while why the Bagget brothers wouldn't leave. They took those brass handles right off the caskets and sold them again.

Anyway, that's how I heard it.

—————

Sonny shone his light on Dad's grave. There were dried oak leaves all over, and Mom brushed them away until it was just the dirt again. You couldn't grow a thing in that dirt, so you brought plants and then took them away. Some people just put plastic, but that never did seem right. As soon as we got some money, we were going to buy Dad his stone.

"Well, I did that one good thing at least," Mom said, her

hand on the small of her back as she stood. After me, her back was never right. "I gave you both a loving father."

It wasn't like the other time. I could tell Sonny wanted to get right out of there.

When he dropped us off at home, I knew where he'd be going all right, but I had to see it with my own two eyes. From our porch, right across from the turnaround tree, I could see about half the Avenue. Sure enough, an hour later, there he was turning around the turnaround tree with Sheila scooched up next to him. I didn't know whether to be glad or sad. I guess I was both, if a person can be both.

6

SONNY SAID he'd drive to the airport, but Mom wouldn't let him, even though she hated to drive. I guess it was because he was going into the Army. She figured he had to be escorted or something.

She began searching for her keys, pulling out drawers, peering under the prep table. She couldn't find them anywhere. I went upstairs to look, while Sonny went back through all the places Mom had already been.

When I came downstairs after looking under the beds, there were the keys sitting on the empty prep table. Sonny came in, then Mom. I handed the keys to Mom. "Where did you find them?"

She stared at the keys lying on her palm. "These aren't my keys," she said. "They're Daddy's."

And then we saw she was right. Dad's had the Welsh dragon.

"They were right there on the prep table," I said.

"But Dad's keys are in his drawer," she said.

We all three stared at Dad's keys with the scratched red dragon on a green field.

"I guess Dad wants to go with us," Mom said, with a lopsided smile.

—————

Mom drove like an old lady, even though she wasn't one.

"Are you sure you have everything?" she said for the sixth time. Sonny said, for the sixth time, that the Army gave you everything you needed. He explained to her that they didn't want you to wear your own clothes. That's what the uniforms were for. She was sure they'd let him wear "real clothes" at Camp Roberts, at least on the weekend. Sonny just shook his head.

Leaving Ojala, Mom had a line of traffic behind her. "Look, Sonny, it's a parade," I said. And Sonny laughed. But mostly he was quiet, and so was Mom. I talked until my words ran out, which took us about halfway to Santa Catarina. Then I got quiet, too. The trouble with quiet is that you have to think, and it wasn't a day when you wanted to do that.

"What if we were going to Canada?" I said, and then I shut up for real.

The radio didn't work. I guess that was good. We'd have argued about what to listen to. Mom said rock and roll rotted the mind.

"You know what you were humming last night?" I said sweetly.

"No, what?"

" 'I Want to Hold Your Hand.' " I waited for her to get it.

"Oh. Well, it's a nice tune."

"It's the *Beatles*, Mother! It's *rock and roll*."

"Oh, no it isn't," she said.

Santa Catarina took twice as long as it should have, which is what happens when you go slower in the slow lane. "This is where we meant to come," Mom said, gazing at the red tile roofs. "It's so charming!" But she was the one who fell for Ojala and made us stay there. "It's so charming," she'd said then, just like now.

It's funny how a turn off the freeway can deal you one kind of life instead of another.

At the exit to the airport, we passed three hitchhikers, long-hairs with peace signs on their backpacks, and headbands like Indians. "My, my," said Mom. But when they flashed her the peace sign, she flashed one back.

"Save your hair, Sonny," she said.

"Huh?" That was unusual for Sonny. He had better manners than that, especially around Mom.

"When they cut your hair," she explained. "Save it in a plastic bag."

"Are you kidding? What for?"

"It's beautiful," she said, reaching across the seat to touch Sonny's wavy dark hair. "You should save it."

"Sure, Mom," Sonny said. "I'll just tell them my mommy wants to remember me just as I am."

"Now, don't get me started again." She pulled some tissue from inside her sleeve and blew. "Don't get me started."

The airport looked like a Mexican restaurant, with striped awnings and pink bougainvillea climbing all over the place. Mom parked right in front.

"Well, I guess this is it," Sonny said, and opened his door.

"Oh, no you don't! We're staying until you leave."

"Aw, Mom." But he pushed the seat forward so I could get out.

"There's Luis," said Sonny. Luis was surrounded by family, a hundred people at least. He wasn't smiling. He looked like he was there to get all his teeth pulled out.

Goose had left the week before, but nobody had heard from him. Goose's real name was Roger and his mother had died when he was a baby. The story went around that when he was twelve, his father gave him his first shot of Jack Daniels and Goose never let up after that. People said that a guy like Goose could do worse than the Army.

There were people lined up inside getting tickets, but nobody else like Sonny and Luis carrying just their duffels and looking like they could be soldiers. It made you think that maybe there wasn't a war after all, that it was only on the TV, and if you believed the TV, well, you were so dumb you might as well join the Army.

The plane was right on time. Luis's family started yelling and crying all at once. Luis was lost in the middle of them and got swept right up to the gate.

Sonny laid his arm across Mom's shoulders. We watched the little blue-and-white plane whir to a stop. Guys in orange jumpsuits ran around getting it ready to go back up.

Sonny had never been on a plane. None of us had. I'd have been nervous as all get-out if it had been me. But I figured some part of Sonny was listening to the plane engine and knew it would hold up.

He turned to Mom and hugged her, burying her whole head in his arms.

Whatever she said got muffled in his chest.

"I'll be fine," he said, and kissed the top of her head. "Don't worry."

Mom was sobbing and hiccuping, as miserable as I'd ever seen her. When Sonny let her go, there was a huge wet spot right in the middle of his pale blue shirt.

"Be good," Sonny said, turning to me.

"Be good," I said, but I couldn't let him go.

He let me hold on a while longer. He patted my back like you burp a baby. "Take care of Mom."

I nodded hard enough for my head to fall off.

I dropped my arms finally. And then I had to ask him one more time. "Sonny?"

"Yeah?"

"You sure you want to go? It's not too late."

His eyes looked so old. "Yeah, I'm sure," he said.

"Phone when you get there!" Mom called as Sonny went

through the gate, swinging the duffel, his tan windbreaker over his shoulder. We watched him climb the steps and bend at the door of the plane, and we waved and waved at whoever was in the fifth seat back. Mom said it was Sonny, but all I saw was a blur.

The plane went racing down the runway and lifted into a perfect blue sky. "Oh," Mom cried, "Sonny forgot his lunch!" I had to keep her from running after the plane waving the Bayley's grocery bag.

We watched the plane until you couldn't see it anymore, just Mom and me, the last two people on earth.

7

THEY CALLED US the day Dad died, said we'd better get there as fast as we could. Something had gone wrong, they said, but they didn't say what.

"Oh, my God," Mom said. "Where's Sonny?" I dialed the Esso with shaking fingers, but Sonny wasn't there. Mom scribbled him a note. "We'll call him from the hospital," she said. "We can't wait."

For once, she drove so fast I held my breath. We ran from the parking lot straight through the lobby, Mom's house slippers slapping the speckled linoleum like castanets.

The door to Dad's room was closed. A nurse stopped Mom from going in. "The doctor's with him now," she said.

"How is he?" Mom was wearing Dad's ugly pea-green sweater with the holes. "Is he all right?"

"The doctor will tell you," the nurse said. She sounded the way nurses do when they've got more answers than the doctors but can't give them to you.

Mom paced up and down, muttering to herself and talking to Dad. I slid down the wall and sat on the floor, holding my stomach so it wouldn't fall out.

Then I thought about Sonny.

"I'll find Sonny," I said, and jumped up. I got all the way to the phone before I remembered you had to have money. I swore, because what else could you do? Then I ran back down the hall to get some change from Mom.

Dad's door was open and Mom was in there, standing next to Dad's bed. She was holding Dad's right hand, the one with the chopped-off thumb, smoothing his arm with her other hand.

She wasn't crying, that was the thing I couldn't get for a while. She looked like she was in love, in real love, the kind you only read about. She looked at Dad like he was made of solid gold, a pharaoh or a king, like he was just the best thing she could ever imagine. She was acting as if he could be reading her mind, which of course he couldn't, not then, not ever.

"Oh, Spence," she kept saying, over and over. "Oh, Spence."

I stood frozen in the doorway, knowing that if I took one step into that room, it would all be true, what I was thinking, what was scratching on the door to my brain, trying to get in. And then Mom just crumpled. Her knees gave out and she went down in a heap.

I guess I screamed because a nurse came running, and then another one. They stuck something under Mom's nose to make her come to. "Cory?" she said, all woozy. "Where's Dad?" And then she remembered. One of the nurses helped her up. Mom put her arms around me, but I couldn't unfreeze. "Dad's gone, sweetie," Mom said, answering her own question. She cradled me against her. Over her shoulder, I could see Dad in the hospital bed. He didn't look any different, except that his eyes were closed. He looked a little older maybe, but then he was lots older than Mom. "Dad's gone, honey."

But he wasn't. He was right there in the bed.

"No!" I yelled, and pushed her away. But when I looked at Dad once more, I knew it was true. He wasn't just sleeping, and he sure wasn't playing a joke.

Mom walked like a sleepwalker over to the bed. She bent over and kissed Dad's forehead, then she kissed his cheek. I watched her the way you watch from the sidelines of a bad dream, there and not there. Mom was being so weird, I wanted to shake her. Dad wasn't supposed to be dead, he just had a cold!

"I've got to find Sonny," I said, grabbing Mom's whole purse instead of the dime I needed. The hallway was like a dream you can't get to the end of. In the booth, I laid my forehead against the cold telephone, breathing the smell of metal. When I could, I dialed the Esso. Sonny was under a Buick. Tell him to come to the hospital, I said. JESUS SAVES, said a sign over the telephone booth, but he wasn't saving us.

I watched the parking lot for Sonny's car, and when it came tearing in I ran outside. Sonny jumped out, slamming the car door. "What happened?"

"He's dead, Sonny," I said. Maybe it wasn't the right way to say it, but I didn't know another way.

"Dad?" Sonny stood there with his arms hanging, like he didn't know what to do with them. "What happened?" he said again. You could see his mind not wanting to get it.

"I don't know," I said. "I don't know what happened."

I followed Sonny inside, down the hall to Dad's room. Mom was sitting by Dad's bed, holding his hand. She looked up. "Oh, Sonny," she said, sighing deeply. That's all. What was there to say? After a while, we left, because that's what you do.

It was all so strange.

But the strangest thing of all happened when we got back home. None of us wanted to go inside, I for sure didn't. Even from the outside, Dad's restaurant looked deserted, the plants droopy, leaves scattered like quick goodbyes all over the steps.

We saw it before the door was open, before Mom pushed it all the way, how the dining room was filled with light. Not sunlight, not candlelight or lamplight, just light. A peach-colored light that we stepped right into, that warmed us like heat. "Do you see it?" Mom said softly, as if words might scare it away.

"Yeah," Sonny said nervously. "What is it?"

"I don't know," Mom said, "but I know it's all right."

All the rest of that day the glow stayed with us and even at night, through the night, the feeling of it stayed.

But in the morning, it was gone.

8

CALLING FROM CAMP ROBERTS, Sonny sounded high. Not like he was on anything, that wouldn't be Sonny, but excited, jittery-excited. Boot camp wasn't exactly fun but they kept you busy, worked you hard, he said, and at night you were so bushed you didn't even dream.

Mom asked him a zillion questions. Did they feed him enough? Cut his hair? Did he know he'd forgotten to pack Dad's Bible? After a while, Sonny asked if I was there.

"I'm on the extension," I said.

He laughed. "Should have known," he said.

He asked me what was happening, who was doing what, as if he'd been gone forever. "Seen Jason?" Then I knew what he was really asking.

I lied. "Nope."

I'd seen Jason, all right. Parked at the Frostee, just like always. Sheila, too, squashed right up beside him in the Deuce. I wanted to reach out and pinch that girl's nose right off.

"Slut city!" Lisa said, but Sheila was the first girl to ride with Sonny in his Ford, if you didn't count me. Even with her bleached white hair all bubbled up, I wanted her to be better than that.

————————

Mom put an ad in the *Sun* saying that the Ojala Café would reopen for lunch. It was a small ad because ads were expensive, but also she didn't want too many people to see it. Without Dad's cookbook, she was flying blind, remembering as best she could what spices he used and how long to cook things.

Saturday would be our trial run. She was going to offer her version of Dad's pot roast, chicken marengo, and spaghetti. But she couldn't decide which of her pies to feature, so she was making all six: apple, rhubarb, peach, pecan, cherry, and custard.

I reminded her that nobody ever ordered the rhubarb, but she said rhubarb pies were cheap and baked two of them. When Sam offered to type the menus, she said she wanted them to be handwritten. Mom was making decisions right and left, like the captain of a ship.

I hoped it wasn't the *Titanic*.

It was my first chance to be a waitress. Mom wouldn't be able to pay me the $1.60 minimum wage, but I was going to get to work every Saturday and keep my tips. In the pocket of my official black waitress apron was a sharpened pencil with an eraser and a new order book with a carbon sheet to slide between the yellow and white copies. The yellow would go to Mom in the kitchen, the white one to the customer. I was nervous but excited, like on the first day of kindergarten when you don't know any better.

"Cory?"

I stuck my head in the kitchen, all the time keeping my eyes on the front door. Mom had flour in her hair. She smelled like onions. Her apron was like modern art. She was holding a bottle of booze to the light. It was empty, except for about an inch. "Where's the rest of this?"

I shrugged. "How should I know?"

She frowned.

"I didn't drink it!"

"Well, it was half full on Thursday when I made the bourbon balls. I was going to put just a drop or two in the pea soup. Do you think Sonny . . . ?"

"Nope. Sonny doesn't drink."

"Well, if that isn't the strangest thing . . ." She stuffed the bottle down into the trash, shaking her head.

———

At eleven o'clock, half an hour before we would have to open the door, Maria came in with a huge bouquet of flowers.

"I carried them out of the florist myself," she said. "Ten dollars for delivery. Highway robbery! Can you find a vase, Cory?" Her face was red and sweaty from walking all the way from her car, about fifty steps.

None of our vases were big enough, so we had to settle for a tin pail. "How avant-garde!" Mom pronounced.

Mom and Maria hugged and rocked the longest time. "I wish you great, good fortune, dear friend," Maria said.

"I'll settle for one smooth lunch," Mom said.

Then Sam showed up with a dozen long-stemmed red roses with a huge gold bow. He looked like a kid at his first prom, hanging on to that bouquet until I wrestled it away. I put the roses in a vase saved from Dad's funeral.

At eleven-thirty sharp, we opened the door and the people poured in like they'd been starving on an island. Two ladies got into a fight over the one window table. Everybody wanted me to take their order first. I didn't know what to do, so I just stood in the middle of the dining room clutching my little order book and breathing fast. I missed my dad like crazy. In two seconds, I was going to start bawling like a calf stuck in mud.

Then Maria made the rounds with the coffee pot, and Sam did some magic tricks with pennies, and I took my very first order. After that, things got easier. I'd take orders as fast as I could, put the yellow copies on the prep table for Mom, and Mom got to work.

Once, she stuck her sweaty face into the dining room and put her hand to her chest like her heart had gone dead. Then she scurried back into the kitchen.

For a while, the people waited like you have to wait for the one good doctor in town. They yakked with each other, then with people at the other tables. But they were hungry, and there were no magazines to read, and so far only one table had food on it.

After a while, they started getting restless—well, you couldn't really blame them—asking me if their lunch was coming, like before *tomorrow*? My face was red and hot and the plates on my arm started jiggling. I watched a plate of spaghetti go slow motion into the pale blue lap of the mayor's wife. She jumped up and screamed, even though the lumpy red sauce that should have been hot, wasn't. I ran to get a towel. Sam said he'd take care of it. Everybody in the restaurant started talking at once. What they were saying, you didn't want to hear.

Then Maria got to her feet. She stood like only a three-hundred-pound opera singer can, and, just like that, everybody shut up. Oh, no, I thought, opera. She flung out her arms and opened her big round mouth. "When the moon hits your eye, like a big pizza pie—"

"—that's amore!" the customers sang, like a trained chorus of barking seals. She kept them going until the food came, and one table after another went quiet and chewed.

"Well, I did my best," Mom said as the last few customers went out the door.

"You did wonderfully!" Sam said. He looked at Maria, then at me. "Well, you did fine," he said firmly, daring us to disagree. But I was the one who had cleared all the half-finished lunches off the tables. I knew.

"I *need* that cookbook," Mom muttered.

9

I WAITED ALL DAY SUNDAY for Lisa to call, then I just gave up and called her. I kind of knew what she'd say, but sometimes you just have to try anyway.

Sure enough, Jimbo was going to pick her up for school, our first day of high school. "Do you need a ride?" she said. She could sound so sweet.

I said my mother wouldn't let me ride with boys yet, even boyfriends of girlfriends, which was sort of true. The subject just hadn't come up yet.

"Well, Jimbo's probably going to ditch, as usual," Lisa said. "So save me a place at lunch, okay?"

I hung up, thinking about what kind of person cuts the first day of school and if I'd want that kind of person for a boyfriend. Well, I wouldn't. But what if that was the only kind of boy that wanted me for a girlfriend? What if I never got a boyfriend at all? There were worse things than not having a ride the first day of high school.

If Sonny were home, he'd have given me a ride. He'd have dropped me off right out front of Ojala High in the Ford on the way to the Esso. I wouldn't have to worry about who I was anymore after that.

I tried not to think about Sonny solving all my problems, but no matter what happened, if it was bad or even only a little bad, I'd hear myself thinking, *if only Sonny were here . . .*

I bought special stationery with smiley goldfish on it and wrote Sonny every day, including Sunday. The goldfish were babyish, but Mom said we should be "upbeat" with Sonny. We should help keep his spirits up. It was hard to write about Jason and the guys and not mention Sheila, especially when I heard they were engaged. Sonny didn't have a real thing with Sheila, but I kept remembering the way his face lit up the night she called, and I just couldn't punch a hole in his spirits.

Sonny wrote once a week from boot camp. Mom and I would read his letters together, out loud, one paragraph each. Then I'd put them in a cigar box under my bed. Anyway, that's what Mom thought. What she didn't know is that, first, I read them all to Dad.

It's kind of weird reading to somebody in a cemetery. You keep looking around to make sure you're alone. You know that if anybody hears you, they will for sure think you are crazy, even if you're only sad. But people didn't visit that cemetery much, maybe because it didn't have grass. I went every day, with or without a letter. I'd take Dad some little thing, like *Blondie* from the funny papers, or a chunk of Hershey's, or a bay leaf. Dad used a lot of bay leaves in his cooking. I figured since the Egyptians offered things to the dead, well why not us? I'd only heard about a hundred and fifty times in eighth grade history that the Egyptians were *a very advanced civilization.*

Of course, if Dad got to take what he wanted like the Egyptians did, he'd have had that wooden casket filled with booze, and I could just imagine what Robert Bagget would have said about that.

I don't know why I didn't talk to Mom instead of to Sonny, who was gone, and Dad, who was never coming back. Maybe it was because Mom would always try and fix things. She'd tell me she knew just how I felt, since she was a girl once upon a time. But the minute she said she knew just how I felt, the thing, whatever it was, would get fatter and fatter, like we were feeding it Wheaties. I just wanted it to go away. I just wanted to hear Dad or Sonny say, "Don't sweat it, Cory." "Don't sweat it" meant that whatever it was wasn't a real problem at all, or if it was, it wouldn't be for long.

I had a zillion worries about high school. For sure, I didn't look right. The whole last year at Ojala Junior, I was late for every class. This was because of my butt. How it stuck out in the back. I had to be the last one to leave every single room, even the cafeteria at lunch. That way, nobody could walk behind me and laugh. (It was okay if I was the last one *in* the room for my next class, that way they were only looking at my front.) I sat through a lot of detention, and Mom got called in to talk to Mr. Land, our principal. He sent me to Miss Martin, the eighth grade girls' counselor. But she had a big butt, too, so I didn't say one thing. I just kept being late.

My butt was the one thing I didn't tell Dad about, Sonny either. I figured since they got to walk behind me, they already knew. Besides, what if I did tell them and they didn't say, "Don't sweat it"? Then I'd know for sure I had a real problem, and that it wasn't going away.

My butt wasn't the only thing wrong, it was just the biggest thing. If you didn't count Lisa, there was the problem of No Friends. Which was not entirely my fault. Practically every person in Ojala had been born there. They got to be friends at about age one. Lisa was everybody's friend, she was that kind of person. But now that she was with Jimbo, all that changed.

It was hard not to sweat that I didn't have friends.

"Sweetie, why are you wearing Daddy's glasses?" Mom looked surprised at first, then worried, as I came downstairs dressed for school. Dad's glasses had come home with his stuff from the hospital, and Mom had laid them on the nightstand where Dad had always put them. They were round with wire rims, John Lennon glasses, except Dad had them first. I'd tried them on for fun, curling them behind my ears. Looking up, I almost jumped out of my skin. Everything was super clear. In the Ireland poster stuck over the bed, I could see the sheep's eyelashes.

The thing is, you can go a long time thinking you are seeing things the way they really are, when you really aren't.

"I need glasses," I said.

Mom cocked her head sideways. "Are you sure?"

"Sure I'm sure."

"Why didn't you tell me?"

When I told her that I didn't know until I tried on Dad's glasses, she looked like I'd stuck a knife in her heart. I guess a mother's supposed to know these things without being told. When I got my period, she looked the same way: knifed. Like she should have marked the calendar and bought the supplies a week ahead. "We'll get you your own glasses, sweetie," she said. "Girl's glasses."

"These are fine." I pushed the glasses up my nose. Some noses aren't meant to hold glasses, which is the kind I happened to have.

"I can't believe my little girl is actually in high school," Mom said, dreamy-eyed. "Are you excited?"

I shrugged.

"Is Lisa coming by?"

"Nope."

"Oh? Are you two on the outs?"

"Nope. I told her I'm not allowed to ride with boys, and she's going with Jimbo."

"Oh," said Mom, biting her lip. "Well, if this Jimbo's *responsible* . . ."

"He isn't."

"Well, then," she said, as if that settled something.

The day before, Mom had cut her hair with the poultry shears because she couldn't find the good scissors. Lucky for her, all it did was curl up around her ears and smell a little chickeny. She looked younger, not so tired and sad. I'd tried ironing my frizz mop, but I had to give up because I couldn't reach the back with my head on the board. Mom, of course, thought it was a dumb idea. "You have lovely curls," she said. "Most girls would die to have hair like yours."

Mom already had her apron on. Once I left for school, she'd start cooking. That way, the pot roast would be real good and done by lunchtime. She was getting better, but business wasn't what it used to be.

"I'm not sure we can make a go of it, Cory," she said. "What do you think about meat loaf sandwiches? I used to make a mean meat loaf, remember?"

"I guess," I said.

"What's the matter, sweetie? Are you down?"

"You sound like Mick Jagger."

"Who?"

"Never mind."

"You're nervous about your first day, aren't you? Well, believe me, I know just how you feel!"

"Oh, Mom, you do not. You do not know how I feel." And I burst right out crying. "I miss Sonny! I miss Sonny so much!" And then I felt guilty. Like I was using Sonny for something he shouldn't be used for. The truth was, I was scared. I didn't know if I could go to my first day of high school alone. People who did that were losers.

"Oh, sweetie, I know you miss Sonny. Of course you do. We all do." Then she thought about that. "We *both* do."

I got up. I picked up my egg-smeared dish. There was no putting it off. If there was one thing worse than the first day, it was being late the first day.

"I smell smoke," Mom said, sniffing.

"Smoke?"

"You know, cigarette smoke."

And then I smelled it, too. Cigarette smoke. Dad's brand.

Ojala High has been around, like, since before the pioneers, or maybe the gold rush. It's nothing special. If it didn't have the sign OJALA HIGH SCHOOL, HOME OF THE RANGERS, what with the bumpy red tiles on the roof and the yellow stucco walls, you'd figure it for a bank. And there's the flag with the grizzly bear on it, of course, right under the American flag.

When you go inside, just in case you go, get ready for a cave, a dark cave. With everybody yelling and banging lockers, crowded in like salmon fighting upstream, you can't even hear yourself think. At first, you are on-the-edge-of-screaming nervous, but then you just give up and start swimming.

This was the major difference between Ojala High and Ojala Junior: at Ojala High, I was flat invisible, from the front *and* from the back. I was just one of the fish.

There was homeroom with Mrs. Shiff, who taught Spanish,

then biology with Miss Furokawa. She was strict, but at least you knew the rules. Third period Spanish was a zoo. Mrs. Shiff was better at homeroom, or maybe the kids were too sleepy to cause trouble first thing in the morning. In Spanish class, everybody talked at once, in two languages.

Fourth period was PE, and since I was never going to take a school shower naked, I got to the cafeteria before anybody else and saved a seat for Lisa by piling my books on the bench.

The caf was nearly full by the time she came. A short chunky girl trailed behind her like a tugboat in the wake of a ferry.

"Hey, thanks for saving us a seat," Lisa said, and made me smoosh over into a sweaty fat kid with a mouthful of macaroni. "This is Melodee, Jimbo's cousin from Visalia. She just moved here. Hey! You're wearing glasses. Cool!"

"Charmed!" Melodee said, and she and Lisa just busted up over that. Melodee had big wet soap-opera eyes and fingernails like Dracula's sister. "Hey, did you guys have history yet?"

Lisa and I would have history together, right after lunch. It was the one good thing in my schedule. We shook our heads.

"Well, wait till you see!"

And then we all did this fishing thing, which is what you do.

Lisa: "What?"

Me: "What?"

Melodee: "You won't believe it!"

Lisa: "What won't we believe?"

Melodee: "When you see this guy!"

Us: "What guy?"

Melodee: "Lawrence."

Us: "Lawrence who?"

Melodee: "The new history teacher."

Then Melodee broke down and gave us the rest. Mr. Dudley, Ojala High's history teacher for about eighty years, had died on the very last day of summer vacation. Lawrence ("Not Mr. Lawrence. *Lawrence*") was the sub the School Board hired while they looked for a real teacher. Lawrence was a real teacher, she said. He just didn't have his credential yet.

"But wait till you see him!" she said, her soap-opera eyes ready to pop. And so we started in all over again.

"Yeah?"

"Yeah!"

"Well, what does he look like?"

"He's tall!"

"Yeah?"

"And he has this, like, wild hair!" Melodee wriggled her fingers like snakes in the air.

"Weird!"

"And he sits on the desk with his legs crossed."

"Is he cute?"

"A *teacher*?"

"Well, you know. For a teacher."

Melodee thought about this. "I guess. Sort of. For a teacher. Except he's real skinny. And he wears Jesus sandals."

"Sandals? A teacher?"

Lisa and I couldn't wait to see this Lawrence. He might be weird, but he was at least something different. The bell rang and we hurried to history.

The room was empty. Maps on the walls, the usual beat-up desks, no teacher. Lisa got the best seat, the last one in the last row, and I sat next to her in row five. First, I read the stuff on the desk to make sure I could sit there for the whole year. *I love Mick*, the usual swastika, *the Beetles Rock*. I thought about correcting the spelling, but I wasn't a desk defacer.

"Hi, there!"

My head shot up and there he was, towering over me like a lighthouse turned on. He was seven feet tall, maybe taller, and skinnier than Sonny, which was skinny.

"Lawrence," he said, sticking out a long arm with a big square hand at the end of it. He wore one of those blue work shirts that looked worn out before you bought them, which they maybe were. There were blond silky hairs on his wrist and three freckles.

It took me a couple of tries to say my name, Corin, my entire first name, don't ask me why.

"Corin," he said, as if it was still in his mouth like a Life-Saver. "Beautiful name. Is it Scottish?"

"Irish," I said.

"Ah, Irish . . ." He nodded like he knew something about me that I didn't even know, something weird or maybe special. His blond hair curled out like rays from the Aztec sun.

Other kids came filing in, taking seats, quiet like you wouldn't expect. Lawrence went around the room shaking hands, like Gulliver wading through the Lilliputians. Kids acted as if they didn't know what their hands were for until that minute. Nobody ever heard of a teacher shaking hands, not with students anyway. That would mean we were grownups, or at least real people, and teachers never thought about us that way.

"How many of you read the newspaper?" He held up his hand, but nobody else did. "Not one? Not even the *Ojala Sun*?"

I raised my hand about a fourth of the way, like a prairie dog sticking its nose up out of a burrow.

"Ah! Corin. One literate soul." He laid his hand over his heart.

"How about the news on TV?"

I would have raised my hand again, but nobody else did.

"Well, here's your very first assignment," said Lawrence, rubbing his big square hands together like a magician over a hat. "Every night, I want you to watch Walter Cronkite or read the front page of the *Los Angeles Times*. Nope, not the *Ojala Sun*. A real newspaper. Okay? Everybody got that?"

I wrote in my new red spiral: Cronkite every night.

"Then I want you to write a paragraph or two about what

you read or what you saw. Got that?" He had a long face, with grooves down his cheeks like Abraham Lincoln. You were ready to trust a face like that right off.

I wrote: Three paragraphs about what I read or see. I was already planning on getting straight A's, like I always got up north. If I wasn't going to be popular, at least I would be smart. Without a boyfriend, I had plenty of time to study.

And then Lawrence slid up on the teacher's desk, crossed his legs, and began telling us about the Vietnam war. It all started a long time ago, he said, with the French. At first, I wrote everything he said, as fast as my hand could go, and then I couldn't anymore. I just stared at his bare toenails and listened, my heart hammering like a woodpecker on a telephone pole. Because it was Sonny he was talking about. Sonny who would be over there in just two weeks. Fighting a war in places that sounded like they should be kid's games, Play Koo, Duh Nang, Chew Lie. When my pen slipped out of my hand and dropped on the floor, I didn't even hear it. Lisa bent to pick it up. "You okay?" she whispered. "You look green."

The bell rang. I was getting a little better about my butt. Still, I wasn't exactly thrilled to walk in front of people, so I waited until last. But here was this new teacher, this teacher who really looked at you, standing behind his desk and saying good-bye to everybody by name. "Goodbye, Corin," he said as I passed his desk, my face burning. But I couldn't call him Lawrence, nobody could, so I just said goodbye and got out of there fast.

At dinner, I told Mom I had to buy a subscription to the *Los Angeles Times* for homework. "Pretty expensive homework," she said. "Can't you just watch the TV?" I said it had to be a newspaper, a *real* newspaper. I felt bad lying because we didn't have much money. Sonny sent his Army money home, almost all of it. Still, with the Baggets and Dad's hospital bill, there wasn't much left. But I knew I couldn't watch the news on TV, not anymore. Not after what Lawrence said about the soldiers and what they had to do. I knew I'd be seeing Sonny's face under one of those helmets, Sonny marching through the jungle carrying a gun. I didn't think Sonny could kill anyone, even if he had to. But what would happen if he had to and he didn't? No more Sonny.

I bought the *Los Angeles Times* at the Ojala Pharmacy and wrote my first homework paragraphs. They were all about the Beatles' *Sergeant Pepper* album.

Lawrence wrote in green loopy letters: "You're a good writer, Corin. Challenge yourself with something more important than rock and roll, okay?"

My next three paragraphs were about Muhammad Ali, who was refusing to serve in the Army. Some people thought he was a hero, but there were others who called him a draft dodger and worse.

Lawrence wrote, "Do you think he's doing the right thing?"

Answering his question wasn't part of the homework, so I just put my paragraphs in my binder and wrote about Twiggy.

Lawrence said: "There's a war going on, Corin."

"Isn't that Lawrence?"

Lisa, Melodee, and I were in the cafeteria at lunch when I happened to glance up and see Lawrence's sunburst hair outside the window. The caf windows were as narrow as the ones in the jail, and almost as high as the ceiling.

"Yup, that's him," Melodee said. "He stands right there for the whole lunch." She crunched a chip, and for once she didn't make us fish. "It's some kind of protest or something."

"Against the war?"

She shrugged. "I guess."

Lisa scrunched up her forehead. "He just stands there?" Lisa's C curls were stuck to her cheeks with Scotch tape.

Melodee shrugged. "I guess."

"What good is that?" Lisa said.

We dumped our trays on the way out, and then walked right past him. But it was like he didn't know us. His hands were crossed and hanging loose, and his eyes were straight ahead. Next to him on the pavement was a sign written in loopy green letters: WAR IS NOT THE ANSWER.

Sonny called after dinner. They were shipping him and his company out the next day. He laughed when Mom asked him if he was trained enough, but I didn't.

10

THE CAFÉ WAS PICKING UP BUSINESS, little by little. Mom even put some stuff on the menu that Dad never would have thought of, like chicken croquettes with garlic mint sauce, and bologna and macaroni. They didn't go over real big, but she was proud of herself anyway, and I guess I was, too. The restaurant had always been Dad's thing. Now she was making it hers.

Mom said I could keep working Saturdays if I wanted to, but school activities came first, and I sure as heck didn't want to miss my first football game, did I?

I was never going to be the kind of girl who went to football games or tried out for cheerleader, but I let her think I was. It was easier that way. Moms need to think those things sometimes, especially if they never made cheerleader themselves.

Or maybe she knew all along I would never be popular, and was trying to keep up my spirits. We did a lot of that, keeping up each other's spirits.

It took sixteen days for Sonny's first letter to come from Vietnam. Mom slit the thin blue envelope open with the bread knife and read the whole thing out loud without stopping, hardly breathing.

———————

August 16, 1967

Dear Mom and Sis,

It's hard to believe, but I am really here in Vietnam, thousands of miles from home. I don't know what I expected to find when I got here, but to tell you the truth it looks a little like Y camp. That should make you feel better, huh Ma? We got tin huts for sleeping (called hootches) and bleachers where they had this lecture first thing about what to watch out for, a lot of stuff. In other words, keep your eyes open. It's a lot hotter than Ojala, wet heat that sticks to you and it rains every day. The leeches are as big as rats, no lie. Food is about what you would expect. The one thing I didn't expect is how beautiful and green this place is, nobody told us about that. They say we'll be doing a mission up-country, but for now it's pretty quiet. Miss you guys already. Try not to worry too much about me. Take care of yourselves. Love, Sonny

———————

"Oh!" Mom said, relieved. "It doesn't sound too bad."

But I kept reading between the lines. What Sonny called a "mission," Lawrence called a "search and destroy." The soldiers would burn people's houses down, which were mostly straw and burned just like *that*. Our soldiers captured what they called the

Enemy, Lawrence said, but they were people just like us. The only difference is that the war was in their country.

Some kids called Lawrence a pinko communist. Jeffrey Marshall asked in class one day if Lawrence had burned his draft card. "I'm a C.O.," he said quietly.

"Yeah? What's that? Communist Organizer?" Jeffrey's father was retired military, you could hardly blame him for being upset.

"Conscientious Objector," Lawrence said.

"You mean you won't go in if you're drafted?"

"No. I won't go in." He sat like a Buddha on the desk, with that same little smile.

Gary Patterson, whose father owned the Esso, got brave then. "Even if they throw you in jail?"

"Even if they throw me in jail. Now who knows what's happening in Washington, D.C., right this minute?"

A half dozen hands shot up, which made me a little sorry I wasn't watching the TV.

"The protest march!" Lisa said. Because of Lawrence, Lisa was getting interested in something besides Jimbo. For the first time in the year that I knew her, she was doing homework.

"Right, Lisa. Tens of thousands of people marching on Washington, our nation's capital, to protest the war. Can you imagine how that looks? You'll see it on the news tonight, but just imagine. *Tens* of thousands. People who don't want this war to go on another day."

"It isn't a war!" Jeffrey shouted.

Lawrence's eyebrows went up and his eyes got bright. "Good for you, Jeffrey! You've been reading. And you're right, technically. This isn't a declared war. But I don't think the bullets feel any different, do you? People are just as dead either way."

"My father says he's going to the School Board," Jeffrey said. "He's going to get you kicked out."

Lawrence looked a little sad for a minute. He got up off the desk and walked slowly to the window. I knew that all he could see down there was a dead agave bush. But when he turned to us, his lights were on again. "Who's going out for the debate team?"

Nobody knew about the debate team, so Lawrence told us all about the school-wide debates, which the seniors usually won. But that didn't mean we didn't have a chance, he said, especially since he was going to be our coach. We would practice debating "the Vietnam . . . *issue*" in class. That way we'd know if we wanted to try out. "We'll start tomorrow," he said. "How about being a team captain, Jeffrey?" Jeffrey shrugged, like he didn't care one way or the other, but I think he felt special. "And Corin? How about you?"

"Me?" The blood shot straight up to my head like mercury.

"Yes. You and Jeffrey will be our first team captains. We'll start by picking teams, first thing tomorrow."

The bell rang. I couldn't move at first. Me? Captain? For a

couple of weeks in fourth grade, I'd been crossing-guard captain. It felt like being responsible for the world, and I was glad when it was over. I stood up and gathered my books, still in shock.

"I think he likes you," Lisa whispered, goosing me in the ribs.

"Who?"

"Who d'ya think? Lawrence!"

My face got bright red and I broke into a sweat. Dad's glasses slid down my nose and I pushed them back up. They were foggy from the sweat.

Lawrence came walking down the aisle. The top button of his shirt had popped off and you could see these silky golden hairs, actual chest hairs. "I'm sorry, Corin," he said, his eyes all sad. "I should have let you volunteer instead of just picking you. Is it all right? Being captain is good experience."

I had this great sudden need to ask him exactly what color his eyes were. I kept thinking about his eyes while I was doing my homework on the Ford Motor Company strike. They were a yellowy brown, but prettier than that. The color of almonds, I decided, toasted almonds. I got so caught up looking at his eyes that I didn't answer.

"Is it okay?"

"Um, yes. Sure."

"Great!" His hand clamped my shoulder like he was knighting me for battle. "Don't tell Jeffrey, but I'm giving him the con side. It's good practice, arguing the opposition. That means your team will argue in favor of the war."

"But—"

"Think about who you want on your team. Probably Lisa, right?"

Lisa shot him one of her cheerleader tryout smiles.

"I'd be proud to have you girls on the debate team," he said. "I hope you'll both try out."

"You see the way he looks at you?" We were plowing down the hall, kids swarming by in both directions.

"Stop it, Lisa!" I was hugging my books so hard they were caving my chest in, which was already caved and didn't need help.

"I'm serious! He just stares at you, even when you're not looking. He's kind of cute, don't you think?"

I couldn't tell her what I was thinking, not even Lisa. Something happened when I was around Lawrence that never happened with any boy, and Lawrence wasn't a boy: he was an actual man. I'd probably written his name a thousand times in my spiral notebook, trying to get started on my homework. *Lawrence. Lawrence and Cory. Lawrence and Corin. Lawrence plus Cory. Cory + Lawrence, 1967–Forever.* Of course, I'd always tear the page into tiny pieces and flush them down the toilet. I didn't want Mom worrying about me and an older man, and if anybody at school found out, well, I'd be done for.

The thing was, I had this overactive imagination and it was causing me trouble right then. If I closed my eyes, I could actually feel how it would be to reach way up there and kiss Lawrence on the mouth. I would actually *taste* his mouth and stars would explode in my belly, and not only there either. I had to make myself just stop it. But then I'd picture him all over again, especially his bottom lip that was fuller than the top one and pillow-soft looking.

"He's *old*, Lisa. It doesn't matter if he's cute."

Lisa scoffed. "He's only twenty-three. He's still in college." She strung her gum out and let it snap back in.

"How do you know?"

"I asked him."

"You did?"

"Sure," she shrugged. "He'll tell you anything. All you have to do is ask."

I thought about all the things I'd like to ask him, starting with his birth.

After school, I went straight to the library. By the time I left, I knew more about the Vietnam conflict than I ever wanted to know. I walked home staring at my feet and almost got hit by a horse trailer.

"We should have gone to Canada," I said to Mom at dinner. She'd heated up the croquettes that didn't sell at lunch. She just wasn't going to give up on those croquettes.

"It's too late to be thinking about that, Cory," Mom said.

"Well, we should have," I insisted. "We should have just made Sonny go. We should have kidnapped him and taken him to Canada."

"What do you think about the new history teacher?" Mom asked. My blood pressure went haywire. I wondered if fourteen-year-olds ever got their heart attacked.

"Why?" There were two hot spots of color on my cheeks, I could feel them.

"I'm interested in your education, Cory. That shouldn't surprise you. I'm a member of the PTA, after all!"

"He's okay," I said, poking through my peas like they were tiny green grenades.

"Well, Sam is on the School Board, you know." I didn't know. "They aren't particularly pleased with Mr. Lawrence's performance so far."

"Lawrence."

"That's what I said. Mr. Lawrence."

"It isn't *Mister* anything. It's just Lawrence."

"That's what you call him? Is Lawrence his first name or his last?"

I told her I didn't know.

"Well, that certainly doesn't seem proper," she said. "I wonder if that's what the School Board is upset about."

"He's a great teacher!" I exploded. "He lets us debate the war. We don't even read the history book. We read the real stuff, like the *Los Angeles Times!*"

Mom frowned.

"If they fire him, I'll quit school. You can tell Sam that!"

"Oh, Cory . . ."

"I mean it! He's the best teacher I've ever had." I was close to tears just thinking about what school would be like without Lawrence.

"Is he?" Mom said gently, her eyes gone dreamy again.

"Yes!" I couldn't look at her.

"Oh, Cory, you've got a crush on him, haven't you?"

I jumped up, knocking my chair over. "I do not! You do not even know what you're talking about!" I fled up the stairs, blood thumping in my ears, and clothespinned the sheets together, the signal to leave me alone.

October 14, 1967

Dear Mom and Sis,

Weather still hot and lots of mosquitoes, but I finally got some net hung up over my cot and so I am sleeping better. We made contact for the first time yesterday out on patrol. It was good to get it over with after so much worrying about when it would happen and where. Don't worry, Ma, your baby boy is no hero. You shoulda seen how fast I dived for the bushes. Then it got quiet, too quiet, *but we moved on. The thing is, Charlie doesn't come right out and fight. He's hiding in the trees, under the ground, just about every-where, ready to make it your last day on earth. Gives you the willies, believe you me. Staff Sergeant says you get used to stuff like this but I don't see how. The guys talk all tough, cuss a lot, but they dive as fast as I do whenever there's incoming (enemy fire). Can't believe I've only been in country one month and already counting the days. It's hard to talk about what it's like in war, but it isn't like I thought it would be. Take care of yourselves and write soon.*

Love, Sonny

I liked doing the debates. Arguing with Mom had been great practice, except for when she cried. Lawrence's eyes would come alive as we made our points and he would pace back and forth, a hand over his mouth to keep from butting in. It was hard to argue in favor of a thing I didn't believe in. How could you believe in something that killed people? But our team was winning, I guess because most kids really believed in the war, just like their parents.

"Don't forget debate team tryouts are Wednesday night," Lawrence said as we left class. "We'll finish up our class debate tomorrow."

By the last debate, both teams were getting sloppy. We'd used up all our good points and were going for scraps. Then Jeffrey stood to make his final summation. "Ladies and gentlemen," he said. "You've heard the saying that a picture is worth a thousand words. Well, this is our final comment on this undeclared war, the *war* in Southeast Asia, the Vietnam *war!*" Slowly he unrolled a poster, and he and Cindy Bellamy held it between them. It was a black-and-white poster, grainy looking, a real photograph blown up. Dead soldiers were lying all in a pile. One had a bare foot, another had his eyes open. The sacred American flag had fallen on the ground.

Nobody said a word for a while, not even Lawrence. Tears slid down my face and dripped onto my desk. The bell rang and nobody moved. Then kids filed slowly out of the room. Lisa, too, like she was in a fog bank. I couldn't get up from my desk. It was like my butt weighed four hundred pounds.

Lawrence shut the door. He turned, surprised that I was still there. He looked as if he didn't know what to do with me. Then he crossed the floor, leaned down, and put his hand on my shoulder. "Are you all right, Corin?"

I shook my head. I couldn't say it, how I saw Sonny in that heap of soldiers. How I was going to die if Sonny did. "My brother's in the war," I said.

"Whoa," said Lawrence softly. "I didn't know, Corin. This must have been so hard for you all this time. You should have told me." His voice was the way cool water feels on your ankles on a hot day at the beach. I picked up Lawrence's hand and held it against my face, cradled it right there under my cheekbone. For a hand so big, it was soft. A heartbeat, maybe two, he let it stay there. He looked into my eyes with this funny little frown, and he let his hand stay right where it was.

Then he took it back and got all business. "Don't worry," he said. "The real debates won't be about Vietnam. The parents don't want it. It'll probably be nuclear energy or capital punishment." He was pulling away with his eyes and his body, and all I wanted was his arms around me. He walked to the front of the room and began erasing the board. I watched his long arm swish back and forth through the chalk dust. I could have watched him bag garbage or pick fleas off a dog.

"See you Wednesday night, right?" he said, dusting his hands together. "You're going to try out, aren't you?"

I nodded.

"Good!" he said. "Great." He stood behind the desk, waiting for me to leave.

11

LISA DIDN'T TRY OUT for the debate team. She didn't go out for cheerleading either, even though she could slide straight down into a split. She'd do it just for fun sometimes, and her miniskirt would go up over her undies. It was because of Jimbo that she didn't go out for anything. If she wasn't in school or at home, she had to be with him. I think this was his rule, but you couldn't really tell since she didn't complain. She even seemed proud, but that didn't make a whole lot of sense to me. I thought the whole point of growing up was getting to do whatever you wanted, whenever you wanted to do it.

Mom was happy I was trying out for a team, even if it was only a debate team. I didn't tell her who was coaching it. Try-outs were easy, since only seven kids showed up and we needed every one. Jeffrey came late with Gary and three other guys who were friends of his. You could tell he expected to be captain again. Jeffrey's success had gone straight to his head. He still didn't like Lawrence, but he loved winning debates.

I was one of only two girls, which gave me more hope than was good for somebody with an overactive imagination. Elaine, the other girl, unlike yours truly, had stick-straight hair and no butt. She never said a word though after the first one, which was her name.

I kept trying to catch Lawrence looking at me when I wasn't looking, which was just not possible.

We practiced after school on Wednesdays. Two extra hours to watch the way he laughed, throwing his head back, getting tears in his eyes sometimes. But if the kids weren't serious about competing, his face turned stony, the way it did when he stood in front of the cafeteria.

Lawrence's new sign read: WAR IS NOT GOOD FOR CHIL-DREN AND OTHER LIVING THINGS. JOIN US IN THIS NON-VIOLENT PROTEST. Miss Furokawa stood next to him, her face in a frozen mask. So now there were two.

That night, I dreamed I had joined the line. Lawrence was holding my hand and smiling. Kids were laughing behind their hands and poking their fingers at us. Well, mostly at me, since everybody knows teachers are already weird. "Don't sweat it," Lawrence said, giving my hand a big squeeze.

I woke right up, my heart playing the bongo on my ribs. Was the dream a sign? If I didn't believe in the war, shouldn't I be doing something? Shouldn't I be standing in front of the cafeteria, too?

Sonny's letters didn't make it sound like he was against the war, but maybe it wasn't smart to be against the war if you were actually in it. I couldn't exactly write to Sonny and ask him what he thought about the war. He might think I was being a traitor, even if I wasn't betraying him, but just the whole idea of the thing. So at noon I walked right past Lawrence and Miss Furokawa, like most of the kids did, as if they weren't really there.

Lawrence kept track of the number of killed-in-action, wounded, or missing on the blackboard, and he kept telling us what was going on in the war, day by day. College students arrested in antiwar demonstrations were losing their draft deferments. Dr. Spock, every kid in the world's baby doctor, got jailed for protesting.

Lawrence wouldn't look at me during his war reports. He probably expected me to start bawling again, which I almost did a couple of times. I'd be the last one to leave class, but he was careful never to shut the door if I was still in the room.

Lawrence went other places to protest, besides our cafeteria at noon. Mom knew all about this before I did because of the PTA. Every weekend there was a teach-in or a be-in somewhere, usually some big city like L.A. or San Francisco, but one time Lawrence went all the way to Columbia University in New York.

I knew about all this, not because Lawrence told us but because Sam told me.

"How's school?" he asked me one Saturday as I whipped

away his empty lunch plate. No matter how much Sam ate, and he ate a lot, including dessert, he couldn't gain weight. Mom said he was lucky. She'd put on five pounds since our grand opening.

"Fine."

I brought him the extra big piece of pecan pie Mom insisted I cut for him.

"What's your favorite class?"

I should have felt sorry for Sam. This is the best he could do.

"History," I said. I'd have said something else if I'd been thinking.

"Good teacher?"

"Yup." I refilled his coffee cup. He was the only customer left from lunch. He was waiting for Mom. If he waited long enough, she'd usually come out and have a cup of coffee with him. After all, she said, he was our best customer.

"Cory? Do you have time to sit down for a minute?"

Well, I did but I didn't, if you know what I mean. "Sure." I pulled out a chair and sat down, crossing my arms on the table.

"You know I'm on the School Board." Sam's glasses were scotch-taped in the middle, a distinctly uncool thing. But his eyes were a clear bright blue, the color of bluies, my all-time favorite marbles.

"Uh-huh."

"And you don't have to tell me anything you don't want to tell me."

I was fine with that. I waited.

"Some of the parents have been coming to our open meetings. They seem to think that your history teacher, the sub, is a"—Sam's bright blue eyes clouded over—"an *unhealthy* influence."

"Unhealthy? Like he's sick?" That was so dumb I almost wanted to take it back.

Sam sighed. He sat back, sort of slumping in his chair. His forehead crinkled, then he sat up again, leaning toward me. I took my arms off the table.

"Cory, I would never do anything to make you unhappy. You or your mother. Do you know that?"

I didn't know what to say. He'd thrown me off track.

I got us back on.

"Are you going to fire Law—our teacher?"

Sam's smile was one of those that only people over the age of fifty can do. It's a smile that says the wearer has just about seen it all, knows everything you couldn't possibly know, and loves you anyway because you are so adorable. "It's not up to me," he said. "I'm only one vote."

"He's a great teacher," I said, feeling the heat creep up my neck in spite of everything I could do to stay calm. "Before him, I was afraid to say anything in class. Now I'm a captain of the debate team. And it's only because of him!"

"Well, yes, I know. Your mom told me about the team. That's wonderful."

But there was more.

"Did you hear about the riots on the Columbia University campus last weekend?"

Well, I was proud to report that I did. I almost told Sam I only read the newspaper because of Lawrence, but he went on.

"Some of the board members wanted to dismiss him on the spot. They aren't exactly in favor of free speech." He saw my face fall and was quick to add: "I wasn't one, Cory. I said we should talk with the students. See what they had to say."

"Oh."

"And you've had some very good things to say."

Tears had somehow gotten into my eyes, and I blinked and blinked to keep them from falling.

Mom came out of the kitchen wiping her hands on her apron. Sam's worried face lit right up. He didn't try to hide his love at all, not one bit.

I started weeping then, who knows why.

"Cory!" Mom said, grabbing my hand. "What's wrong?"

"Nothing," I said.

Mom and Sam watched me with matching hopeful looks, ready for anything I had to say about the awfulness of being a teen. They'd been there, their faces said. They knew.

Ha.

The School Board broke down and said they'd give Lawrence another chance if he'd cut his hair. He didn't cut it. Instead, he wore it pulled back in a ponytail, tied with a leather cord. It just made him look more serious, more dedicated to changing the world.

———————

Dear Mom and Sis,

Thanks for all the good birthday stuff. Especially the comic books, Cory. You read my mind, only I didn't want to sound like such a kid by asking for comics. The guys can't wait to get their hands on them. I've got the Oreos and the malted milk balls hid or they would be gone in two minutes flat. Things going okay here, not much action in the last couple days, but you are always listening. Nobody wants patrol, but you feel like hell if somebody else gets hit, so you might as well be out there looking for Charlie. The worst thing about patrol is the elephant grass, sharp as a knife and about twice as high as me. You can't see if the VC are in the middle of all that grass with an ambush. My hands get pretty cut up. Well, the worst thing about patrol isn't the grass so much I guess, it's the fear. Nobody talks about it, but you can see it in all the guys' eyes, no matter how long they've been here. We are being moved out, closer to where there's supposed to be more action. But we will get some needed R & R first. Will write when we settle. Take care of yourselves. Happy Thanksgiving. Save a drumstick for me. Love, Sonny

———————

Mom invited Sam and Maria for Thanksgiving dinner, but without Dad and Sonny it wasn't close to the same. As we ate our overcooked turkey, a cold hard rain beat against the windows and leaked in under the French doors. Mom watched it come in like she was in a trance, so I mopped it up with a towel and pushed the towel against the door.

Sonny was going on a lot of missions, but that's all we knew. "Went out again yesterday," he said. Or: "We're going out more often now."

"At least he's getting out a little," Mom said. For once, I kept my big mouth shut. If she didn't know what missions were, I wasn't about to tell her. Our TV never went on until after the news. Then it was *Bewitched* or *Bonanza*. But my homework paragraphs had changed. Now I wrote about what was happening in Southeast Asia, not only Vietnam but Cambodia, too. Or I'd write about what was going on at home, on college campuses like Berkeley, where the kids hardly went to classes because of all the protesting.

Lawrence always asked how Sonny was doing, and once I read him one of Sonny's letters. "He sounds fine, doesn't he?" I said hopefully.

Lawrence looked at me for a minute as if he was trying to decide what to say. "He sounds like he's in Kansas," he said.

"Where?"

"Kansas." Lawrence sighed. "He's trying to make it sound not so bad," he said. "For you. Especially for your mom. That's what they do. It's bad, all right. You shouldn't fool yourself about that."

And then, one day at lunch, without even thinking very much about it, I stepped into the protest line. Which really was a line now, with four teachers and three students. The students, all girls, weren't the popular ones, and now they never would be, but they looked like they didn't care about that. They looked like they cared about Children and Other Living Things. I was sure Lawrence loved each and every one of them.

It was strange to look out from that line. Nobody poked their fingers at us. They tried hard not to see us, but their eyes would sometimes give them away. If I didn't know better, I'd have thought they looked scared.

Lawrence never said a thing about the line. He just stood there for thirty-five minutes, which was how long our lunch was. Then he'd come walking into history, slide up on the desk, and start the class. Lisa asked if he'd said anything to me that first day when I stood there shaking, wondering what I was doing, seeing life from the other side. He hadn't said one thing, which was better than if he had. I knew the deepest things were always said without words.

Christmas came and went. We didn't have a tree. Sonny's gifts got mailed the month before, so they would get there in time. I made Mom a coffee cup in ceramics, but the handle came off in the kiln. We used it as a sugar bowl. She gave me a mohair sweater. It was the exact color of Lawrence's eyes, which how could she know? On Christmas day, we lit candles for Dad at Saint Thomas Aquinas. Mom said it was okay with God for Protestants to light candles in a Catholic church. I wasn't real sure she was right. But the church was beautiful, with all the statues shining in the candle-light and Saint Thomas on guard in the front.

"I don't know why we don't go to church anymore," Mom said, walking home. "Why don't we start going again?"

"Where? Saint Thomas?"

"Why not?"

Sometimes she would sound more like a person than a mom.

"You want to be a Catholic now?"

"Well, maybe. I love that little church, don't you?"

"Well, sure. But you just can't get up one day and just *be* a Catholic." Sometimes my mom didn't seem to know all the rules, I don't know why, since she was almost forty years old.

"Well, I don't know why you can't," she said. "I think it should be entirely up to a person what he or she believes. It's a simple matter of conscience." She did that little head-cock thing, like she was on her high horse, as Dad used to say.

But Saint Thomas helped us get through Christmas, and I was grateful to him. He might have helped us find Dad's cookbook for all I know. It was right there on the prep table when we got home, a book so old it no longer had a title.

All I could do was stare at it, while goose bumps raced up and down my arms.

But Mom grabbed it right away. "Well, it's about time!" she said, and began flipping through it. Then she got real quiet, turning the pages slowly. That's when I saw how Dad had written on nearly every page, filling the margins.

"Look at this," Mom said. I squinted my eyes to make out

the letters: *Corin's sixth birthday. Made the lamb. Appetite like her father. Next time, not so much pepper.*

Mom turned the page and there was *Christmas 1957: crown roast, scalloped potatoes, French string beans, Parker House rolls. The family healthy, life good.*

———————

Sonny's letters changed after Christmas. It wasn't a thing you could put your finger on, Mom said, but I could. Sonny didn't sound like Sonny anymore. He'd let things leak through in words that weren't Sonny's, or didn't use to be Sonny's. "Sweeps" and "trip wires." A Cobra was a helicopter with guns, not a snake. The good people were ARVNs, the bad ones were NVA. The lieutenant got "fragged," he said, and now they were waiting for a new one. Lawrence said that meant the lieutenant had been shot in the back by his own men, but Mom wouldn't believe that our boys could do something like that. "It sounds more like hazing," she said. "You know, like fraternity pranks. I'll bet that's what he meant. You don't shoot your own leaders. What kind of a war would that be?"

Debates were set for the third week of January. To Lawrence's surprise, the topic was "Vietnam: An Unwinnable War?" The idea came from Walter Cronkite, who'd said exactly that on the national news. He made a lot of people angry because it threatened morale. But he made people start to think, too. If we couldn't win, why stay another day? The *Sun's* editorials urged peace and reconciliation and get-out-quick. People began taking their flags down, and soon there were just a few left.

After all we'd done on *that* topic in class, Jeffrey said, we hardly had to practice. Even though Jeffrey was voted captain for the school-wide competition, Lawrence said his attitude was exactly the wrong one to take. Lawrence stepped up our practice, promising a pizza party on the last night. "We'll beat the pants off them!" he said.

Elaine blushed. She blushed whenever anybody said a word that had to do with body parts or sexual activity. Even when the word had a clear other meaning, like "balls" or "missionary," she'd light up like a Chinese New Year.

After practice, I walked Elaine to her mother's car. "Let's exchange phone numbers," I said. "In case we want to practice extra, or something." I felt sorry for her because she was so quiet, but I wasn't exactly Miss Mouth in school either.

"MaybeYouCouldSpendTheNightSometimeAtMyHouse. WeCouldSleepOutsideInMyTent!" Elaine said without taking a breath, her face as pink as cotton candy.

"Sure," I said. *Sleep in a tent?*

With her pen she wrote my phone number on her hand, so I wrote hers on mine. It wasn't exactly a blood bond, but it was close.

Lawrence was late for practice. We figured he'd stopped to get the pizza, but when he came in, no pizza. Something was wrong, you could see it on his face. He stopped just inside the door and looked at us, his big square hands riding his hips. Then he slumped into the room and sat down in one of the kid desks, his knees up to his chest. "North Vietnam has launched a massive attack," he said.

"Well, so?" Jeffrey said. "We'll just hit them with everything we've got!"

"Maybe," Lawrence said, his voice hollow. "Maybe we will."

"And maybe they'll just win and the war will be over," I said.

Lawrence looked at me, and I knew there was something he stopped himself from saying. "It's a bad situation," he said. "It's just a bad situation."

"Hey!" said Jeffrey. "You promised us a pizza!"

"Whoa!" Lawrence said, slapping his knee. "You're right. I was watching the news, and, well— Okay! Let's go then!"

We followed Lawrence outside. His VW bus was parked right in the middle of the parking lot, not between the lines. There were no other cars, but still it seemed strange to see it sitting there. It was a happy-looking kind of bus, covered with peace signs and flowers and ocean waves.

"Sorry, no seats in back," Lawrence said, as kids climbed in. "Grab a pillow and make yourself comfortable."

"Hey, it smells like feet!" said Jeffrey. "You live in here or what?"

"Pretty much," Lawrence said.

I waited to be last, so I could sit in the front. There were beads dangling from the rearview mirror and a necklace with a peace sign. The seats were torn a little on the shotgun side, so you couldn't help but sit close to the driver.

The bus wouldn't start at first. Lawrence cranked and cranked it, and I could tell just from that he didn't know a thing about engines. I thought about Sonny's Ford and Jason's Deuce and how far I'd come from that world. I didn't want to think about what Sonny would say about how the bus smelled, but I guess it *could* have been incense and not what I thought.

At last the bus started and Lawrence chugged out of the lot, the engine backfiring and threatening to stall.

We had our pizza at Papa Tony's and, for once, we didn't talk about the war. Lawrence told us about how it was to go to college, and about how proud of all of us he was. We were smart kids, he said. We knew how to use our heads. I was proud of us, too. Everybody but Jeffrey was in the protest line now, and Elaine and I were starting to hang out.

When we were back in the bus, Lawrence asked the kids where they lived and began dropping them off. Elaine was next to last, and then there was me.

"Eat a good breakfast!" Lawrence called as Elaine, waving back, went up her driveway. "See you in the morning!" Elaine's house was at the top of a hill. We waited until the last speck of her white blouse disappeared into the trees.

Then the engine died. Lawrence started cranking it again, but it wouldn't start. He was just going to flood it, I could have told him that. But I didn't want to sound like I knew stuff about cars. I didn't think he had much respect for cars or his would be in better shape. When I smelled the gas, I knew I'd been right.

"We'll have to let it sit awhile," he said.

"Okay," I said, and then my overactive imagination got the best of me. I slid all the way across that seat.

"Corin?"

"You can call me Cory," I said, but I could hardly catch my breath for all the butterflies crowding my throat. "Everybody else does."

"I like Corin," he said.

I thought he'd make me move over, but he didn't. We just sat there looking out the window for a little bit, like we were at a drive-in movie. It was dark as the peat bogs in Ireland, which I only knew about from hearing my dad talk but which I knew were very dark. Thinking about my dad made me so sad, but sitting next to Lawrence warmed my heart. I didn't care if he thought I was a slut, which I could never be, having not the least little bit of experience. I'd kissed two boys in my whole life, and only one of them touched my chest for about a minute before I slapped him off.

I laid my head against Lawrence's arm. It felt like the right thing to do, even if it wasn't, like picking up his hand that time and putting it against my face. Lawrence lifted his arm and put it around me, so easy, as if we'd done it lots of times. The smell of his armpit, which wasn't exactly fresh but the armpit of a grown man, made my head spin. He had to be hearing my heart, it was knocking so hard. I turned my face up and there my lips were, just inches from his, our warm breath mixing. I'd already decided not to close my eyes when he kissed me. That way, I wouldn't miss a thing.

Lawrence leaned closer, his face like the moon getting bigger, his lips parted. Then he stopped, just stopped in midair. Sighing, he laid his head back and closed his eyes. When he opened them again, he gently pushed me away.

"I love you," I said into my lap, the three little words I'd practiced a hundred times in my daydreams. I didn't dare look at him.

"I love you, too, Corin." I could hardly believe my ears. Was I dreaming after all? But when I looked up, all I saw was this crooked little smile, and I knew. "Of course I love you. You're a very special girl. But it isn't . . . it isn't"—he sighed through his nose—"*that* kind of love."

"Because you're old? I mean, older than me?"

"I'm your teacher, Corin. It's not right. If the School Board saw us here—"

"Who cares about the School Board?" I blurted out, needing a target. "Who *cares* about them?"

"I do," he said quietly. "I love teaching, Corin. They could make sure I never taught again, anywhere."

"Oh." The air went out of me and, with it, all my courage.

"This is a hard time for you," he said softly. "I know that." I wanted him not to talk, not to say anything if all he could do was sound, well, like a *brother*. "If someone I loved was in this war, I probably wouldn't be as brave as you."

"I'm not brave," I said, miserable. "I'm scared all the time."

"Bummer," he said, shaking his head. "That's a real bummer." Lawrence rolled down his window. The singing of the cicadas brought back the night when Sonny left the Ford in my care, and I hadn't even washed her once.

"It's hard for your folks, too, I'll bet."

"Yeah."

I couldn't tell him about Dad. What kind of a person loses a dad and a brother in less than one year? A loser, that's what kind. Even though my head knew it wasn't my fault, my heart didn't always.

"If something happens to Sonny . . . if he gets wounded, or . . . *you know*, would they tell us right away?"

"They try to," he said. "They do it in person, if they can, which is decent."

"They come right to your door? The Army?"

"Right to your door," he said.

"Like the Avon lady."

"Like a letter bomb," Lawrence said, with more bitterness than I'd ever heard. Then his voice got gentle again. "I know how much you love Sonny," he said. "You're a girl full of love, the purest, best kind. But Corin?"

"Yes?"

"You've got to save a little of that love for yourself."

He started up the bus. "Do you understand what I'm saying?"

I mumbled something that must have sounded like I did.

Lawrence drove us back to town, talking about tomorrow's debate, which didn't matter to me then as much as it was supposed to, as much as a kiss would have.

When we passed the Frostee, I waved to Jason and Sheila, but they didn't wave back. They probably couldn't imagine knowing anyone who would be riding in a car like that.

12

IT WAS A NEW YEAR, almost. First Jason would have to make it official by driving through Ojala at 110 miles an hour at the stroke of midnight. He'd been doing it every year since he was sixteen. The first couple of years the cops chased him, then they just gave up and cleared the streets instead. Now it was this big community event, with people lined up along the Avenue like the Fiesta parade was coming.

I promised Mom I'd go to Saint Thomas Aquinas with her the next day, a Sunday, if she would stay up and watch Jason's run with me. All we had to do was walk to the corner. She didn't see the use in staying up until midnight to watch something that lasted just a couple of minutes, which is the way grownups think, so I wasn't exactly surprised. But I worked on her awhile, and she finally gave in.

To keep her from changing her mind, I refilled her coffee cup a bunch of times after dinner. Soon she was yakking a hundred miles an hour, folding three weeks' worth of napkins and refilling all the salt shakers. Then she found some big band music on the radio and made me dance with her, twirling me around and around until, breathless, I begged her to stop. Dad would have loved it, Mom and me dancing and laughing.

Still, it made you a little guilty. Wherever Sonny was, I didn't think he'd be laughing. And Dad? Well, that depended, I guess, on where he was.

At ten minutes to twelve, we went outside, into the chill of the year's last night. The moon had shrunk to nothing, but strung along the Avenue were kids with sparklers and grownups holding candles stuck through paper cups. People tooted party favors or blasted car horns, as if they just couldn't wait to get the old year over with and start a new one. I could understand that.

"Listen real hard," I told Mom, "and you'll hear Jason's engine."

"Okay," she said, but I could see her mind was somewhere else.

"Cory?"

"Yeah?"

"What do you think about Sam? You like Sam, don't you?"

I liked Sam, but I didn't like the sound of this.

"Because he wants to take us to Disneyland."

"Disneyland?" I scoffed. "We're too old for Disneyland. Anyway, you two are, for sure."

"Well, Sam says, since we've never been . . ."

Mom was wearing the red velvet slippers I'd given her for her birthday. What with Disneyland, and all, it made you think about Dorothy on the yellow brick road. As I was getting older, Mom seemed to be getting younger.

"I don't know, Mom. It's weird. I think he just wants to have a date, and this is the only way he can get you to go."

She thought about that. "Well, I suppose you're right."

I tuned my ears into the distance but didn't hear Jason. I bit down and asked Mom the crucial question: "You don't like him, do you?"

"Sam? Of course, I like Sam."

"You know what I mean. I mean do you *like* him?"

"Cory! Of course not. Like a man, you mean?" The way she looked, you'd have thought we were talking about aliens.

"Are you sure? Because, if you did, I don't think Dad would be mad." This seemed like the grownup thing to say, and I almost meant it. Sam had saved Lawrence's job. He listened to what kids had to say. He was old, and he wasn't cool, but a mom could do worse.

For a couple of minutes, all she could do was blink and think. "Oh, Cory, I don't think I could. Date, I mean. It's way too soon." She was using her hands as braces again, so I knew she was having trouble with her back. "I'd just like to, you know, have some fun once in a while." She gave a little punch of a laugh, like you do when you're laughing at yourself. "I guess that seems strange to you, huh?"

It did, but in a way it didn't. The restaurant was open on the weekends for dinner now, and soon would be open for business every day and night but Tuesday. Mom had Patsy and Karen working again, and Patsy's son, Don, was the busboy, but when I'd overheard her saying she still worked twelve-hour days, I couldn't believe it. Then I counted. She was right.

"So how about Disneyland?" she said.

I shrugged. "Sure."

"It's been a hard year," Mom said. The way she said it was like an announcement to God not to do it to us again.

From a long way off came the song of Jason's engine. "There he is!" I said. "Hear him?"

Mom listened. "No . . . Oh! Yes! I hear something!" Her eyes lit up like a kid's.

People began to cheer as the Deuce came howling out of the dark at the other end of the Avenue. I hoped people were holding on tight to their kids, because Jason wasn't going to stop for anything, not even a road block. They'd tried that already and he went right through it, blowing the wood to smithereens.

I grabbed Mom's arm and pointed. "See his lights?"

"Yes! Come on, Jason!" Mom yelled, waving her arms like the cheerleader she never got to be.

And then it was over. Jason screamed past us in a shiny black blur and was gone. Shouts and cheers all down the Avenue. Happy New Year, they yelled. And then, just like that, it was 1968.

Mom put her arms around me and hugged me hard. "Happy New Year, Cory," she said.

"Happy New Year, Mom." It was good to hug, even if she smelled like fried onions.

I wrote Sonny about Jason's run, because I knew he'd want to hear all about it. But Sonny didn't write back. I'd hit the mailbox like an attack dog, but all we got were bills.

Mom was sure Sonny was fine. "I could feel it if something happened to him," she said. "I would just feel it in my heart." But she looked worried just the same. Then one day, when she put salt instead of sugar in the apple pie, I knew her mind was not on business.

Weeks passed. It had been hard going to the cemetery in the winter. What with all those gray stones and bare trees, the cemetery looked like a movie made in black and white. I'd sit there wishing we could afford to buy Dad's stone. Mom said first the hospital bill, then the Baggets, then the stone. But it was sad. Even with the plant from the jail with a star stuck on top, it didn't look like we cared.

Sam took Mom and me to Disneyland. At first, I tried acting my age, but then I just gave up and had fun. Sam loved all the scary rides, just like me, and screamed right out loud like a girl.

In case you think so, fourteen is not too old for Disneyland.

Sam had been a perfect gentleman, Mom said when we got home, which meant that he'd passed his first test. But he had a long way to go with Mom, I could tell. If it weren't for Dad, I'd have felt sorry for Sam. He was like a good dog trying to please a cat.

———————

January 17, 1968

Dear Sis,

Sorry about not writing but we have been on the move. We have seen a lot of action, which I don't want to scare you about, but it's the truth. Don't tell Mom but things are pretty bad right now. Thanks for writing so much. When I get mail I almost feel normal for a little while and like I might get out of all this one of these days. Fighting a war isn't anything like I thought. Lots of days, nothing goes on and you get so bored. It's funny, you wouldn't think a war could be boring, huh? But then we get incoming and all hell breaks loose. We were hit by a bunch of mortars day before yesterday. Buddy of mine's leg got it bad and they had to take it off. Probably shouldn't tell you this stuff. I've just been thinking about how we used to talk. Well, me and my big mouth. But try not to worry about me too much, Sis, because I'm going to make it out of here so I can give you lots more grief. Took these pictures on R & R. The guys with me are Tim Oakes from Kansas City and Billy Bo Brandt from Memphis, Tennessee. Everybody takes their pictures with guns, hope that's okay. Hug Mom for me. Take care of yourselves. Love, Sonny

———————

After all our hard work, the school-wide debate kind of fizzled. Not because we weren't prepared. We were *too* prepared.

Nobody knew as much about the Vietnam war as we freshmen did. Even the seniors sort of gave up after a while and let us win. But Lawrence said we'd done a great job, which is all that really mattered, at least to me.

Goose was coming home. He'd been wounded. Bad. That's all we knew, because that's all his father seemed to know. His father was passed out about half the time and sleeping the rest, so nobody could get all the facts.

Jimbo started collecting the orange crates for a bonfire even bigger than the last. Goose loved a party, and this one would be all for him, even though there were other things to celebrate, like Jason and Sheila's engagement and Jimbo's birthday. Jimbo would be turning eighteen, which wasn't such a good thing now. No way would Jimbo get into college, so it was just a matter of time before he got drafted. He wasn't worried about it. He'd do his two years, get himself some "gooks," come back with the Purple Heart. He had John Wayne daydreams, Lisa said.

But all that ended when Goose came home, when Jimbo went to meet him at the Greyhound bus station, when the bus driver got out, set up the wheelchair and carried Goose down the steps of the bus. After that, Jimbo was quiet.

The party started after my ten o'clock curfew, so Mom wouldn't let me go. From our porch, you could see the fire blazing and, through it, the bell tower of Saint Thomas Aquinas, reaching into the night sky. I tried to feel sorry for myself. I said, *if only Sonny were here.* But I didn't really care anymore about the bonfire parties. I wasn't even fifteen, and already I'd outgrown that kind of thing. What would Lawrence think if he came by and saw me dancing like an idiot around some stinking fire? Not that he *would*, but if he *did*, by some chance, drive by or something. He would lose all respect for me, respect that I was hoarding like silver, hoping it would turn into the gold of true love.

I'd convinced myself by then that he looked at me when I wasn't looking. I'd feel this special kind of heat against the side of my head or on my ear, but I could never turn fast enough to catch him at it.

Every day at school he'd ask if I'd heard from Sonny, and when I shook my head, he'd shake his, too. It was a thing we shared, something nobody else had.

It had been so long that I could hardly believe my eyes when I caught a glimpse of blue among the bills on a Tuesday afternoon in March. I ran into the restaurant and up the stairs to where Mom was trying on a pantsuit the exact color of baby spinach, turning in the mirror so that she could check out her butt. It was normal, but she checked it out anyway. It was strange to see a mom in pants, but I said she looked very hip.

"Too big in the hips?"

"No," I said. "Cool. Guess what! We got a letter!"

"Oh, my gosh! Read it, read it!" Mom sank to the bed like her knees got unhinged. I sat beside her and peeled open the folded Army stationery. If you weren't real careful, you could rip right through the writing and maybe miss the most important stuff.

March 5, 1968

Dear Mom and Sis,

*Sorry for not writing but I have been laid up. Could not hold anything in for too long and they finally sent me to the hospital.
Dysentery is what it is. I am down to 160 but starting to pick up
a few pounds. You can't believe how good clean sheets can be, with a
real pillowcase, too. I've been sleeping just about all the time. Got to
talk to a chaplain, told him about my dreams, how scared I am all
the time (you don't tell anybody else, but a chaplain is okay). He
said I'm no different from anybody else. Everybody's scared WIT-
less (ha!). Nobody wants to be here. But how would this war go if
everybody just refused to fight it? Well, then the war would be over,
I said. He thought I was being a smart mouth, but I wasn't. Another couple of days here and back to business. If you can, please
send some Instamatic film and more comics, okay? Take care of
yourselves. Miss you. Love, Sonny*

"They should send him home!" Mom said, incensed, when
I'd finished reading. "He's sick!"

I shrugged. "At least he can't die in a hospital." And then I
thought about that. "Can he?"

"Oh, I don't think so. No, of course he won't."

"But what about Dad? They said he wouldn't die."

Mom's eyes got this faraway look. "Your father didn't take

very good care of himself, Cory. He drank too much, and he smoked so many cigarettes . . ." her voice trailed off.

"Well, you can't take care of yourself in the war either," I muttered.

Mom lifted my chin and looked deep into my eyes. "You used to have such a sweet disposition, sweetheart. Don't let all this war stuff change you. Sonny will be fine. I know it." She gave my chin a little squeeze.

"It isn't just Sonny," I said, thinking about Lawrence, shaking loose of her hand. "War is wrong, Mom. It's wrong for our country to be there." And then I went on for a while, like Lawrence doing his Buddha on the desk, while Mom listened, her face growing more and more troubled.

"I still think you're too young to involve yourself this way," she insisted when at last I wound down. "And have you taken a good look at yourself lately, young lady?"

She turned me so that I was facing the mirror. I took the good look she asked me to take. My hair was long, still frizzy because I'd given up on the ironing, but I wore it back now, tied with a leather cord. It made my face look more grownup, even with the freckles and Dad's owly glasses. A bead necklace with a peace sign hung down over my orange-and-green tie-dyed shirt. "So?"

"Don't you think it's time for a little makeup? Some mascara? A nice soft pink lipstick?" She smiled encouragingly over my left shoulder like a dope dealer.

"Nobody wears makeup, Mom."

"I do. Am I nobody?"

How does a kid answer a question like that?

"And those pants, those bell-bottom things. They're too long. They drag behind you. Just look at this hem!" She reached down and took hold of the shredded bottom of one pant leg. "Your clothes look like they came from the thrift shop."

I shrugged. "They did."

Her eyes widened. "Do you mean to tell me that you spend the money I give you for clothes at the thrift shop?"

"What's wrong with that?"

She thought about it. "Well, there's nothing exactly *wrong* with it."

"That's where we got the stuff for the restaurant," I reminded her.

"But *clothes*," she said. "Other people's *clothes*. I don't know . . ."

"When you buy new clothes, you support the Establishment," I said.

"The what?"

"The Establishment. You know, like"—and then I realized I didn't really know how to explain—"*everything!*"

Mom looked doubtful. "You're not a hippie, are you, Cory?"

"Of course not," I said hotly. "Of course I'm not a hippie."

13

"WHO'S THAT?" Lisa stopped at the door to history, flinging an arm like a crossing guard. I peered in over her shoulder.

A gray-haired man was sitting in the swivel chair behind Lawrence's desk, his back perfectly straight. Through the glasses perched on the end of a long pointy nose, he was reading our names on the roll sheet.

"Oh, my God," I breathed. "Do you think he's a sub?"

"For a sub?" she said. "A sub for a sub? I doubt it."

"Lawrence is sick," I said. "He's got to be." I hoped whatever he had wasn't serious, but I truly did hope that Lawrence was sick. If he wasn't sick, that meant he was gone.

We took our sweetest faces inside. The gray-haired man looked up with his gray eyes. They were kind eyes, but that didn't matter, not to me, not one bit. He did not belong in that room.

"Excuse me, sir," said Lisa. What she wanted to say was "Where the hell is our teacher?", which would have been pure Lisa. Instead, she said, "Is Lawrence out for the day?"

The gray-haired man stood. He smiled and did this almost-bow thing. "Good morning, girls. You're a bit early, aren't you? I was just looking over the roll. My name is Mr. Pritchard."

"Is Lawrence—" My voice had climbed an octave and all my cells trembled.

"I am your new teacher," he said.

"But is Lawrence—?"

"Yes, I will be replacing the substitute who was taking Mr. Dudley's place, as you know, after Mr. Dudley passed on. I'm glad you two are early. You can help me pronounce a few of these names." He picked up the attendance sheet.

"Excuse me," I cried, and fled.

"Cory?" I stared at Lisa's feet on the other side of the stall door. She was wearing the sandals that crisscrossed all the way up to her knees. It wasn't right to have those legs and not use them for anything worthwhile, like drum majorette or at least girls' softball. "You all right?"

"No."

Why hadn't Sam told me? What if he hadn't even tried to save Lawrence this time?

"Well, you can't stay in there all day. The bell's about to ring."

"Go ahead and go," I said. "Tell Mister What's-His-Name that I got my period or something."

"I will not! Are you crazy?"

"Well, tell him something. Tell him I died."

"Oh, it's not *that* bad."

"Easy for you to say. *Mother!*"

"Well, just think," she said. I watched her foot arch, so I guessed she was checking out her toenails, which she still polished. Her feet were her best feature, she said. Talk about nuts. "Now that Lawrence isn't a teacher, maybe you have a chance. Did you think about that?"

Right then, I wondered why I ever thought Lisa wasn't the smartest girl in the whole school. I opened the door.

"Besides, I happen to know where he'll be this weekend." She cocked one perfectly arched eyebrow.

"Where?"

"In Santa Catarina. There's going to be this big peace rally at the university Friday night."

"Mom would never—" Then it hit me. Destiny. The café had sprung a major leak and was closing for repairs. Maria was treating Mom to an opera weekend in L.A. They'd be leaving late Friday afternoon. "Are you guys going to the rally? You and Jimbo?"

"Jimbo? At a peace rally?" Then, seeing my face fall: "Well, I could try to get him to take us."

I gave her a quick hug and we raced to class just as the bell rang.

———

Maria was picking Mom up at four. It was five till, and Mom was doing this Cher thing with her eyes. It took a very steady hand and about ten minutes, start to finish. She was wearing black knee-high boots and a skirt that was pretty short for a mom. "Are you sure you're not going to L.A. with Sam, and not Maria?" I teased, my face behind hers in the mirror.

"We don't lie to each other, Cory. You know that." My stomach did a double-flip and my eyes glazed over. "Do you have a pair of really warm socks I could sleep in? The hotel might be cold."

"Sure!" I said, grateful for the chance to escape. I rummaged through my underwear drawer until I could remember what she asked for. Was it true we never lied? What about white lies? Fibs? Maybe she didn't tell me any, but I sure told her some. Things were getting complicated, when all I had was one thing on my mind.

Why hadn't he said goodbye? That was what I just couldn't understand. If Lawrence thought we were so *smart*, if he thought I was so *special*. Goodbyes were important, especially for somebody who didn't get one when she needed it from the one person in the world she needed it from the most, her father.

But Lawrence didn't know that. He knew that I loved him though. He knew that, because I'd told him. I wasn't sorry either.

Lisa hadn't called, so I figured she was still working on Jimbo. "I'm going to wash Sonny's car," I said, tossing the socks on Mom's bed. "Have a fun time!"

"Cory? Did you leave me Elaine's phone number?" It was

going to be my first sleepover at Elaine's, a serious step in a friendship.

"Oh! Yeah! I'll put it in your purse."

Which anybody could forget to do between going down the stairs and backing a car out of a garage to wash it.

Sonny's car started right up, even though I forgot to do it every week. I decided to Turtle Wax her after her wash, to make up for past neglect.

When Maria drove up and honked her horn, Mom came running out with her little overnight case. " 'Bye, sweetheart," she called. I waved goodbye. How could a person feel so many things at once and not just explode with them? I was glad to see Mom go. Now I could stop thinking about the lying thing, which wasn't exactly a lying thing, since I *was* going to stay at Elaine's when she first told me about her trip. And I didn't say that I *wasn't* going to a peace rally. That would have been a full-on pitch-black lie. But it still didn't feel right somehow.

And, besides, Mom and I hadn't been apart for a night since Y camp. There was a lump in my throat as I watched Maria's car drive off. Could a person grow up a piece at a time? If that was true, then you could have throat lumps and still be maturing. After that, I felt a little better.

I called Elaine and cancelled our sleepover. She sounded disappointed, another thing to worry about. Maybe she wouldn't want to be my friend, once she thought about it for a whole night.

Then Lisa called while I was feeding Feckless bites of my hot dog. Jimbo wouldn't go to a peace rally if you held a gun to his head, she said. Which didn't make a lot of sense but said all you needed to know about Jimbo. "I'm sorry, Cory," Lisa said. "Want to go cruising with us instead?"

I said no, thanks. I'd just go up to Elaine's, I said. Her mother was gone, too, so we could do just about anything we wanted. I didn't know what that could be, even in imagination, but Lisa didn't have to know that. I was going to that rally to find Lawrence, if I had to crawl the thirty miles on my knees.

But I knew how I was getting there all right. I didn't want to think about it. I didn't even really want to do it, but I had to. I had to see Lawrence. I had to be close to him again, even if it was just this once. I had to let him say all the things he would have said if he'd gotten the chance. Our lips had gotten so close, I was sure if they got that close again, nothing could stop them. He wasn't my teacher anymore. I clung to Lisa's words like George Harrison with a mantra: he wasn't my teacher anymore. I would remind him of that, in case he'd forgotten.

14

TURTLE WAXING A CAR isn't as easy as it sounds. I'd done my best on Sonny's car but there were streaks all over it. Sonny would have polished the Ford until the primer spots shone, so I worked on it some more, which wasn't so good. Polishing gave me too much time to think about what I was going to do. Sonny's keys were in my pocket. The Ford was shining ready. It was easy to slide right in and start her up.

Tying the dark scarf over my hair was the final thing, no turning back.

I drove hunched forward, my hands sweaty and my heart knocking so hard I had to gulp for air. If anybody'd got a good look at me, they'd have thought that old lady with the scarf was about to have a stroke. But only a few cars passed, the people inside them minding their own business.

Once before the freeway, I had to pull over to wipe off Dad's glasses. Those glasses would fog up at the worst times, just when you needed to see things the clearest. I got back on the road, put my hands at ten and two, the way Sonny had taught me, and headed for the on-ramp.

This was the scary part. I'd been gathering cars behind me like a funeral all the way from Ojala. And suddenly there it was, the sign for U.S. Highway 101. I remembered how it was from driving with Mom and Sonny. The road took this little curve, and there you were all of a sudden on the freeway, going sixty-five miles an hour. Only I was going twenty. The cars behind me started honking, but I couldn't make my foot push harder. Cars zipped past on the freeway like a slot car game. I had to do it. I had to get up my speed and my nerve. I pushed the gas. The Ford said, Yes! I cranked my head around to get a good look at what was coming, and a Mack truck the size of a billboard went barreling past, air horn screaming. I closed my eyes and jumped in behind him.

I drove the freeway like Mom, slow as the turtle the wax was supposed to come out of but really didn't. After a while, I started to relax. The freeway was cinchy. The hard part of driving was having to do the clutch with the gear shift at the exact right time. On the freeway, all you did was push the gas and steer.

It took me until almost dark to get to the university. Being a criminal is easier the darker it gets, and so I got to breathing and acting normal. I even took my scarf off. I thought: if breaking the law was this easy, no wonder people did it all the time.

Where the students lived was like a little town, but basically it was a dump, broken-down cars and bicycles all over the place. You could find an old couch any time you needed one by just driving down the street. Trash was everywhere. I guessed the university didn't think kids needed clean streets, or else they couldn't keep up with all those students using all that paper.

I drove slowly into the heart of the place, which was four corners of pizza, burgers, coffee, and Chinese. Kids streamed along the sidewalks or rode their bikes, all in the same direction. Some were carrying signs saying STOP THE WAR and PEACE OR ELSE. I crept along beside them, trying to keep Sonny's big engine quiet. Up ahead was the People's Place, a vacant lot with scrubby grass. That's where all the kids were headed.

There was no place to park, cars along every street, some with flat tires and about a hundred tickets stuck under the wipers. Then I spotted the church. UNIVERSITY METHODIST said the sign in the middle of a neat little lawn. I drove right in like a customer.

Churches are a little like Chinese restaurants. You can always find one when you need it.

The lot behind the church was empty, so I picked the number three spot for luck. Then I got scared and couldn't open the door. Something told me I should drive right out of there the way I came, but I couldn't do that. Lawrence was close, I could feel it in my bones, or in my heart, I guess. I thought about saying a prayer, seeing as I was already behind a church, but it didn't seem right, praying for a kiss from an ex-teacher.

After a little while of bouncing back and forth between the right thing and what I wanted to do anyway, I got out. I closed Sonny's door quietly and locked it. Then I pushed his keys way down into my backpack so they wouldn't get lost.

The night was so clear you could see the face of the moon as it inched up the sky. Lawrence said that a man would go up to the moon one day, but it was hard to believe anybody would want to. And what if they couldn't get back? What if they were a Russian? What if they were a woman? I wondered if everybody got these thoughts that didn't match the occasion, or if it was just me. Then I started thinking about what was normal and what was not normal, which could make you crazy, so I stopped.

Stuffing my sweaty fists into the pockets of my jacket, I headed for the People's Place, whistling through my teeth to keep my spirits up. They were sinking fast. What with all the people, how would I ever find Lawrence? Already the People's Place was filled with people. University kids—there were regular people, too—had brought blankets to sit on and were passing around wine bottles and food. On a rickety-looking bandstand, a kid was trying to do Jimi Hendrix without an amp, but nobody was paying attention. Hanging over everything was the smell of marijuana, what Mom called "the devil weed." You could get a contact high if you sucked the smoke in, so I tried to breathe with just the tops of my lungs. That way, I could say that I tried not to get high and even if it happened, I wouldn't be lying.

Lies were piling up like pickup sticks. If one got loose, the whole mess would come down.

I sat on the steps leading up to the stage and looked over the crowd of heads for the one special one. In our classroom, Lawrence had seemed so different, *was* different, but not here. There were guys with hair longer than his, wearing faded blue work shirts and beads, raggedy jeans with rope belts, Jesus sandals or no sandals. But not one of them was as tall as Lawrence. Not one of them smiled in that gentle kind of sad way, as if he knew you better than you knew yourself.

After a while of people talking and passing things back and forth, a guy with a big bare belly and pigtails got up on the stage and announced the speaker, "straight from the center of the storm at the University of California at Berkeley!" The crowd whistled and cheered as a man leapt onto the stage from the ground. He had the face of a pirate, with black flashing eyes and a wild mane of black hair. He wore a beaded vest over nothing at all, and washed out jeans.

"Brothers and sisters!" he yelled, grabbing the mike that sputtered and crackled. "What do we want?"

"Peace!" said a few voices scattered through the crowd.

His hand cupping his ear, the speaker yelled into the mike again, louder this time. "I can't hear you! *What* do we *want?*"

"Peace!" came the roar.

"When do we want it?" *Shree-ee-ee* went the mike.

"Now!"

"What do we WANT?"

"PEACE!"

"When do we WANT it?"

"NOW!"

I sat on the steps hugging my knees as waves of sound came crashing against the stage and into my stomach, the words blending until it was one hollow, echoing voice.

WhatdowewantPeaceWhendowewantitNowWhatdowewantPeace
   WhendowewantitNOW!
WhatdowewantPeaceWhendowewantitNowWhatdowewantPeace
   WhendowewantitNOW!

At last, he stopped asking. More cheers and whistles. People clapped, yelled out stuff to show how mad they were about the war. A yellow dog came running up to me, his tail wagging. It felt good to let him lick my face, but he did it to everybody who let him. A love dog, Dad would have said. Not like Feckless, who only really loved one person: Dad.

The speaker started talking then in a regular voice about what was going on with some people called the SDS who were in Berkeley, but other places, too. They were students, I figured that out, but it didn't sound like they were doing much studying. Then he told a horrible story about our own American soldiers killing dozens of people. Not only men, the speaker said, his voice kind of crooning, but women and children, too. Old people. Innocent people, we probably would never know for sure how many.

The crowd went quiet, like they were all breathing one hurtful breath after another. Tears made people's faces shine. Mothers hugged their children to them, as if they saw themselves over there in Vietnam standing in front of those guns.

I clung to my knees, not wanting to believe such a thing could be true.

Then the speaker heated up again, his voice getting louder as his fist punched the air. American corporations were backing this war, he yelled. Dow Chemical made the napalm that turned people into human torches. There was a Bank of America right in the middle of Saigon. And then they were chanting again, the pirate and the crowd.

"What do we want?"

"PEACE!"

He jumped down from the stage and the huge speakers started blaring the Stones. People got up and began milling around, loose and restless. There were shouts, angry shouts, and then the crowd started collecting, moving like one big slow animal toward the middle of town. I stood up and watched them pass, looking for Lawrence.

And then I saw him, or thought I saw him, way on the

other side. I stepped down into the crowd and tried to move toward him, but there was no way to go but the way the crowd went. I held my head up to breathe and got carried along. An older man tripped and fell. A couple of people tried to help him but were pushed on. "Lawrence!" I cried, but my voice got swallowed up in the rumble of voices and chanting. I told myself it was just people, just people that's all, but I felt the panic rising like it did the time I almost drowned at the YMCA. It was just people, but nothing in the world, except maybe guns, could have stopped them. They didn't even know where they were going, but it didn't matter.

I tried to get out by going sideways, then I tried to stand still so the crowd would move around me, a stone in the river. But I kept going forward, sweaty bodies knocking into me, boozy breath all around until I wanted to scream. I knew if I fell, they would go over the top of me as if I weren't there. It happened at rock concerts. People died that way. I felt these little chuffs come out of me, *huh, huh, huh,* and knew then that I was crying.

Whatdowewant?Peace!Whendowewantit?NOW!Whatdowe want?Peace!Whendowewantit?NOW!Whatdowewant?Peace!When dowewantit?NOW!Whatdowewant?Peace!Whendowewantit?NOW!

At last there was air and some space. The crowd slowed and, like spilled marbles, rolled off in all directions. A kid reached down and picked up a rock. I watched him throw it in a perfect baseball pitch toward the music store. A window crashed and fell into the street. People cheered. "And it's one, two, three, what are we fighting for?" Country Joe sang from the speakers in the People's Place. "Don't ask me, I don't give a damn. Next stop is Vietnam!" People sang along like at a party: "One, two, three, what are we fighting for?" Then it was the Stones again, singing about a street-fighting man. You could feel things change with the music, heating up.

The crowd began to collect around an old barbershop, one that still had its red-and-white striped pole. Only now the barbershop recruited soldiers. It said so right there on a sign: UNITED STATES ARMY RECRUITING CENTER. Across the window somebody had scrawled the F-word in red paint that dripped like blood. The center was dark and closed, since it was nighttime, but people started chanting anyway, to let the Army know how they felt. "Stop the war! Stop it now!" But the energy was gone, I guess because nobody was home. After a little while, people started moving away, some back toward the park, others toward the open stores.

I heard a loud rumble and whipped around. A dumpster had gotten loose. It was rolling straight at me. I jumped to the side. Then I saw the two guys who were bent forward, pushing it. The dumpster was rolling so fast, they were practically running. One guy was short and hefty; the other was tall, his hair loose and flying. Above his head he held a flaming torch made of newspaper. It was Lawrence.

Other people had heard the rumble, too, and were coming back toward the Recruiting Center. "*Lawrence!*" I screamed, but he didn't hear, or couldn't hear. I watched him touch the torch to what was inside the dumpster and a blaze shot up. Then there were others pushing the flaming dumpster. They were pushing it straight toward the windows of the Recruiting Center.

The crowd swarmed around me so that I couldn't see. I heard the crash of glass. A roar went up from the crowd, silhouettes against an orange glow, and then I saw the flames leap up, sparks snapping and flying, as the building caught fire. I pushed to the front with strength I didn't know I had, and there, in a haze of smoke and flame, was Lawrence, his hands on his hips, staring up at the fire leaping higher and higher until the girders of the roof dripped metal like rain.

I started to run, coughing, dodging through people as they stared dumbly at the fire. I couldn't think. I had to get someplace where I could stop and think. My mind was a swamp of thoughts that I couldn't sort out, didn't want to sort out. I headed for the People's Place. On the other side of that was the church and Sonny's car.

I heard a chopping sound, faint at first, then growing louder, filling the night: *thwack-chop, thwack-chop, thwack-chop.* I spun around, turned my ankle on a bottle. Pain shot up my leg. Coming down out of the night sky like a giant grasshopper was a helicopter, SANTA CATARINA COUNTY SHERIFF in white letters on the side, heads with dark helmets, shotguns. "Clear the streets!" said the voice of God through a bullhorn. "Clear the streets immediately or you will be arrested."

Some kids were crying as they ran. Others stood their ground, yelling back at the helicopter, punching the air or holding up their middle fingers, as if that could do anything. Suddenly everything turned to smoke. My eyes began to itch and water. Somebody yelled, "Tear gas!"

Dad's glasses slipped off and hit the ground. I dived for them, but it was too late. The glass in one side was a spiderweb of cracks. I put them on, peering through the smoke and that one good eye for my landmark, the steeple of the little church. All I could see were the ghosts of people scattering in all directions. Somebody's big hand grabbed mine and pulled me, stumbling, through the crowd. I didn't care where I was going then, I just ran. The hand let go. The air cleared and there was the church.

It wasn't until I saw Sonny's car that I began to cry. It was almost as if it was Sonny himself waiting. I fumbled through my backpack for his keys, terrified that I'd lost them somehow, along with other stuff I couldn't name but felt.

I opened the door and climbed into the backseat. I locked both doors. Then I curled up and lay there listening to the sirens, afraid to close my eyes, afraid to move.

It got light without me knowing, so I guess I slept. A bird was singing, a mockingbird I knew it was, because it could do all these different songs without having any of its own. I wondered if it wanted to have its own song, or whether it wasn't just easier to copy another bird's song instead.

Did it matter if you didn't have your own song?

These were the kinds of questions that seemed important, even if no book could answer them. Important or not, I couldn't seem to stop myself from thinking them up.

I opened my eyes. It was any old morning for that bird, but not for me. I lay there and listened for sirens and helicopters, but all I heard besides that bird was the screech and bang of a garbage truck. I peeked up over the window ledge. There was nobody around. The one end of the People's Place that I could see was empty.

I got out of the car holding my back like Mom.

Was it all true? Nothing in my life had ever seemed so much like a nightmare. But the air smelled like smoke, so I knew it was true.

Still, I had to see for myself.

A sheriff's car passed and I ducked behind a hedge. I hadn't done anything bad, except for driving without a license. Which was bad, sure, but not like burning down a building owned by the United States Army. Still, I tried to stay out of sight. The sheriffs might think I was returning to the scene of the crime, which I was. Only the crime wasn't mine, it was Lawrence's.

I shook my head, trying to replace that picture of him running behind the dumpster with one of him sitting on the desk, telling us about how wrong war was, about nonviolence and how we had to live together in peace, his hands resting quietly in his lap. I kept remembering how he'd carried a spider all the way to the window one day in the middle of history and set it outside on the ledge. He did it without thinking, without stopping what he was saying, as if he saved living things every day of his life. I remembered how he'd stood so still in front of the cafeteria, his face like stone, his hands crossed like he would wait there forever for things to be right in the world again. How could that Lawrence be the same Lawrence I saw last night?

But it was. No matter how hard I tried to convince myself that I'd seen a Lawrence look-alike, I knew better. It was the fierce look in his eyes that I couldn't forget. Not because it was so different, but because it was exactly the same.

15

AFTER THE PLUMBERS LEFT, I cleaned the kitchen with my conscience and, boy, did it sparkle. I almost went back and messed up a few things, knowing how smart moms could be, how they could torture a weak conscience and make it talk.

Scrubbing the grungy old linoleum, I thought about how a restaurant could become a home in spite of you. I thought about lots of things, about Dad and Sonny, about Mom and me and how different we were now, more like friends than mom and daughter.

But then I sort of changed my mind about that. Like for instance if I'd have asked to go to the peace rally or asked her to take me. No way. She was still a mom and I was still fourteen. That wouldn't change until my birthday, and maybe not even then. Which was sort of good. Dad said if you didn't put up a fence, sheep were so dumb they'd keep right on going to the end of the world.

Not that I was a sheep, or dumb, but I *was* a teenager.

I didn't want to think about Lawrence. I searched my mind the way you poke a stick through a dead campfire, trying to figure out how I felt about him now. I knew it wasn't the same. Had I fallen out of love? That was the $64,000 question. Could a person fall out of love in just one day, over just one thing? What kind of person would do that? If a person could fall out of love that fast, over a single thing, maybe that person was not really in love in the first place. But that was the worst thought of all. Almost kissing him had made me dizzy, actual fall-down dizzy. If that wasn't true love, what was?

I thought about kissing him now. Same thing. Same dizzy. It didn't make sense. But then I thought about Bonnie and Clyde, how they truly loved each other, and they were both criminals of the worst kind.

And then I began to miss Sonny, and then Dad, and then Sonny again. After a while, I cried myself out. Lawrence never loved me. He'd told me so, only I didn't want to listen. And now I was in love with a criminal.

I polished Sonny's car again. I counted the hours until Mom would get home, twenty-eight. I counted the months until Sonny would be home on leave, four and a half. I called Lisa, but she wasn't home. I didn't call Elaine. Our friendship was still in the baby stages. The way she blushed about body parts, well, she probably wouldn't want to be friends with a criminal.

I decided I would go to Saturday mass. I would light another candle for Dad. I would pray to keep Sonny safe, and I would pray for Lawrence, too. Only there I was stuck. Should I pray that he didn't get caught?

This was the thing: Could a person who was mostly good do a really bad thing and still be good? Could a person be good one day and bad the next, and then good the day after that? Could a person who was good to children and spiders but bad to the American government still be considered a good person? And then what about people who lied and drove without a license?

This is the kind of thinking that gets you going to mass.

It was one of those shiny days that stick in your mind long after, the air as clear as good TV reception and the sun blazing down. I stuffed my scarf in my pocket and headed for the Avenue. Mom and I had been the only women in the church with bare heads that first time, which was extremely embarrassing. Why they didn't kick us out, I don't know.

At first, I didn't want anybody to see me. Church wasn't exactly a thing you talked about. It wasn't cool. And anyway, here I was doing the wrong thing again, breaking the rules. I was supposed to be a Protestant, but I didn't feel like a Protestant. I didn't feel like a Catholic either. I just felt like going to church. When Jason and Sheila cruised by, I waved. Sheila started to lift her engagement hand, then I guess she thought about it and changed her mind. Maybe she was a Catholic and guessed where I was going. Maybe she was just a jerk.

I crossed the street. Then, with a block to go, I slowed my

steps. Up ahead, parked along the Avenue, was a line of black cars. I saw Robert Bagget get out of his limousine and stride into the church. The dirt lot across the street was filled with cars parked in straight lines.

Even though I wasn't wearing black, nobody stopped me. I walked alongside a family and I did what they did, dipped my fingers in the holy water and, when I didn't drop dead right on the spot, crossed myself top to bottom, left and right. I knelt when the family knelt, and sat where they sat, up near the front.

The smell of incense was as strong as marijuana in the People's Place. I thought about that, how one kind of dried plant could be the devil's weed and the other kind God's. I wondered where all that got decided, and how it got decided. Did people sit around a big table somewhere—say, Switzerland—and go through a list of good and bad plants, and then make the rules? Indian tribes had their own rules about herbs and plants. Were those rules just as good as ours?

It made me crazy sometimes that I didn't know stuff. I was beginning to think a person could go their whole life and not know everything. It was a little like getting a license to drive without knowing all the rules, and wasn't that kind of dangerous?

Saint Thomas was the boss of that church, but Mary was the most beautiful. She wore a long white dress with a pale blue veil draped over her head. Her fingers were thin and graceful-looking, and she held one hand up a little ways, like Jesus did, as if to say, "Wait. Listen." It made your heart tremble.

The priests, all in white-and-gold, moved back and forth on the stage as if they were on rollers, the kind Sonny laid on to get under the cars. There were vases of white lilies and tall white candles burning. A casket like Dad's, that same golden brown wood, was half-open. From the pews, you couldn't see the face inside, which I thought was good.

In the next row up, a woman in a black hat and veil turned her head to the man beside her and I saw that it was Mrs. Moreno. At first I didn't get it. All the beauty of the church, I guess, the glow of the candles, the chant of prayers going back and forth between the people and the priest. I wanted to ask somebody whose funeral this was anyway, but how could I do that? I was supposed to know, that's why I was here.

Old people died all the time. I pictured an old man in the casket, Luis's grandfather, but Luis kept popping into my mind, how he bounced the backseat of Sonny's car like a kid, how he always saw the bright side of things.

After a while, the front row stood and started filing out. I watched them shuffle along, then stop and look into the casket. Some were crying, mostly the women, with men holding them up. Mrs. Moreno reached in and laid her hand there for a while. She didn't want to go, and kept looking back.

Our row was next. I was herded along for the second time in two days, only this was different. I could have turned away, nobody was making me go. Shuffle, step, shuffle, step. Closer and closer to the casket. It was lined with pale blue satin, the color of Mary's veil. I looked around the side of the man in front of me and saw hands. Young hands. Light brown. Young hands, crossed. And then I saw Luis. *Luis dead?* No one told me he was dead. Maybe I wasn't paying attention. My mind had been somewhere else.

He looked like a little boy sleeping, his long eyelashes curled against cheeks that were paler than Luis's, but Luis's just the same. I knew how death was, how silent death could be, but still I wasn't ready. When it came to be my turn, I felt like I was suffocating and kept sipping little breaths of air. I wanted to say something to Luis, even if he couldn't hear it, and so I said, "Goodbye, Luis." It was all I could think of. Tears were streaming down my face. I'd cried so much in one year, it made you wonder if a person could run out of tears, and if that was the reason why some people didn't cry at all.

I walked to the cemetery, knowing the way like nobody else in that town. By the time I got there, Luis was already in the hole and the Baggets were filling it up, waiting for the people to leave so they could snatch those handles.

I watched from Dad's grave, telling him how sad it was to see somebody that young being put into a grave. It was sadder to see your own dad put into a grave, of course I told him that, but I think Dad knew what I meant. All over our country, boys were coming home in black plastic body bags with zippers. It wasn't right and, now, even the senators and congressmen were saying so. Mom said that when Robert Kennedy got to be the President, he would stop the war for sure.

Sonny wasn't writing much, and when he did, his letters didn't sound right. "Mom and Cory," he wrote, not dear anybody. "Not much to report." As if we wanted a report! I tried to read Sonny's voice into his words, but I no longer could. It scared me that in such a short time the sound of his voice in my head could be lost. I'd wake up in a cold sweat sometimes, my heart going bonkers. Did my heart know something I didn't? Had Sonny been shot? Was he dead?

Sometimes, when I couldn't get back to sleep, I'd crawl into bed with Mom. It probably set me back a little in my maturity, but right then I didn't care.

Mom came back from L.A. all rested and happy. She went on and on about some opera where everybody died in the end, which she said was "absolute perfection." Sometimes Mom didn't sound like Mom either. Maybe I wasn't sounding like me anymore, but how could I know that unless somebody told me?

She asked if I'd had a good time at Elaine's, which I dodged as fast as I'd dodged that dumpster. "Luis Moreno got killed," I said, and told her about the funeral. We both got quiet after that. I knew what Mom was thinking because I was thinking it, too. If Luis, a boy we knew, a boy who lived right here in the tiny nowhere town of Ojala, California, could die in the war, well then, anybody could, even Sonny.

After dinner, we drove over to the cemetery. Mom bought some roses for Dad and some for Luis, whose grave was heaped with fresh dirt. Mom laid the roses on the top, and we stood there awhile. Then we went over to Dad.

"I think we'll have enough for the stone next month," Mom said, brushing away the dried leaves, but suddenly I didn't want a stone. Not yet.

"Let's wait until Sonny's here," I said.

Mom said okay, right away, which is how I knew she was reading my mind. If we waited for Sonny, Sonny was sure to come home.

The phone rang as we walked in the door. Mom answered it. "It's Sam," she said. "He wants to talk to you."

I glared at the receiver, then I took it. "Hello."

He jumped right in. "Cory, I wasn't there. I missed the School Board meeting when they took the vote. Of all meetings to miss! There wasn't anything I could do. I'm so sorry."

"It's okay," I said. Sam didn't know it, but we weren't talking about the same Lawrence anymore.

"It is? We're still friends?"

"Friends," I said.

Mom was waiting as I hung up the phone. "Well?"

"Can't a girl have a private conversation around here?"

"Uh . . . sure," she said uncertainly. "Well, of course she can!" As if it had never occurred to her to ask in the first place.

The funny thing, for a mom, is that she never wondered what happened to my glasses.

On the fourth of April, Martin Luther King, Jr., was shot and killed in Memphis, Tennessee. Mr. Pritchard said we would have five minutes of silence in our classroom to honor one of the world's great champions of peace.

I wanted Lawrence to be there that day. I wanted to hear what he'd say about Martin Luther King, about nonviolence, which was what that great man gave his life for. But Lawrence was gone, gone with the wind, which was funny but not so funny. Lawrence was like a force of nature that blew into our lives for a while, then blew right out again. Like the hot winds of August, he'd stirred us up, leaving his mark. I didn't think I would ever see him again, and still I wanted to.

16

NOW THE TALK was all about peace. You would think that's what they had in mind from the beginning, President Johnson and all those politicians. Sam, who was teaching me how to play chess, said it was an unpopular war all along, and that the protest finally wore our leaders down.

Sam and Mom were doves. But there were still plenty of hawks around, Maria for one, who said all this peace talk would just get more of our boys killed. It was better to sound strong, and then kind of sneak on out of there when nobody was looking. Sam said it was just a matter of time and the war would be over, either way.

I thought that without Lawrence the protest line would fall apart, just like the debate team did, but you didn't dare drop out as long as Miss Furokawa was standing there with her frozen face at 11:55 every single school day. It made you ask yourself the hard question about why you joined the line in the first place. Was it Lawrence or was it the war? I decided it was the war. I hated it. I hated that it took Sonny and that it killed innocent people. I looked out from that line and just dared anybody to get into a debate with me. I may have been the captain of the pro side, but I knew the con argument better than Jeffrey. For Jeffrey, the whole thing had been a game. He was just as much a hawk as ever. But I was a dove, a pure white dove.

It was finally June, just seventeen days until summer vacation. Sonny would be home in August. Two months away. Sixty days. One thousand four hundred and forty hours. He hardly wrote at all. I told myself it was because he was coming home so soon that he didn't think it mattered, but two months wasn't exactly soon.

It had been a while since I wrote him every day on the happy fish stationery, but I still wrote a lot. Finally, I had to tell him about Jason and Sheila. They were getting married at the end of August. I couldn't have him coming home and stepping into that like a pile of dog poop. Sonny said to congratulate them. He didn't sound like he cared one bit.

Someday I would write a book, *How a War Can Change a Life.* Maybe I didn't know a whole lot of history, but I sure knew what could happen to regular, real live people. Then I started thinking again. What if a person wrote a whole book, with chapters and all, and it didn't change one other person's mind? Was it still worth writing?

Mom came into my room. It was the middle of the night. I felt her nudging my shoulder, saying my name. She was crying. I sat straight up. "Sonny!" I almost screamed it.

"No, no, sweetheart. Oh no, I'm so sorry. I shouldn't have woken you up. I just didn't want to be alone. It's Robert Kennedy," she said, wiping her eyes.

"Robert Kennedy? The brother?"

"He was shot, Cory. They don't think he's going to live. It was at some hotel in Los Angeles . . ."

I hugged Mom while she wept. Secretly, I was glad it wasn't Sonny. Maybe it was wrong to think such a thought at such an historic time, but I couldn't help it. I felt sad about Robert Kennedy and I felt especially bad for the eleven children who wouldn't have a father anymore, but the closer we got to August, the more scared I got. I was freaked about telephone calls, the mail, and especially if Mom was crying.

Was life all about death? What kind of a deal was that?

———

Mom and Sam were going out on dates now. She didn't call them that, and when I did, she got furious. They were "just friends," she said. Women could have male friends. A woman didn't need a man to take care of her anymore. A woman without a man was like a fish without a bicycle.

I thought she made that up until I saw it on a T-shirt.

I didn't know how to tell Sonny about Mom and Sam, so I didn't. She could do it herself. If she could look Sonny in the eye and tell him she and Sam were "just friends," then I guess they were. I told Dad, though. I told him straight out that I thought Mom was dating again. And then I listened as hard as I've ever listened, but I didn't learn a thing.

Sometimes I just felt like the last person in the room after the lights got turned off.

Elaine was moving to Vermont. Her father was some big shot in this secret government organization that she didn't even know the name of. Thanks to this secret organization, I would have to start all over with friends in the fall.

Except for Lisa. She was still a friend. She was a real good friend whenever she and Jimbo broke up, which was about once a month for three days. I had Lisa like I had my period, except she was of course more fun.

Ninth grade ended like a party that never happened. No graduation, like in eighth. We just sat around on the lawn signing yearbooks, or waiting to see if somebody would ask you to sign their yearbook, so that at least you could tell if you were the most unpopular kid in the whole school or not. You could sit a long time like that, especially if Lisa was ditching. So, on the last day, for no reason at all except that I wanted to, I asked this guy to sign my yearbook. He was one of those kids who could go through a whole year in class without saying a word, without hardly even moving. He'd been in my Spanish class, but I didn't think he could speak the language. You had to open your mouth for that.

His name was Burt (kids called him Burp) and if he wasn't the most unpopular kid, he was close.

"Hi, Burt," I said. "Would you please sign my yearbook?" I held it out like a peace pipe. He looked at *The Ranger* like he didn't know what it was. Then he looked up at me through his Buddy Holly glasses. His eyes were the exact color of pale green Easter eggs, if you dip them in for just a second.

"Uh, sure," he said.

"You can sign anywhere." I shrugged. The ninth grade was all in one picture. Some faces were lighter, some were darker, but you could hardly tell one pinhead from another.

He scrunched down over the yearbook with his pen like a chicken laying an egg. Then he handed it back. "I don't have one for you to sign," he said.

"That's okay," I said, all breezy, like somebody popular. "Thanks!"

I went around like that for a while, asking everybody I saw who wasn't with somebody to sign my yearbook. There weren't that many. Asking for signatures wasn't any different than trick-or-treat. Being popular was a lot like wearing a costume.

I couldn't wait to get home to read what they'd written, even though I didn't expect much. After all, nobody knew me.

"Good luck to a real nice girl," said Alicia Muñoz. "Class of '71 rocks," said William E. Fisher, Jr. "Stay cool. Love, Dave." "See ya in the fall!!" said Linda Lee Blinkerman in purple ink. "Thanks," wrote Burt. His handwriting was so crimped I could hardly read what was underneath his name. It looked like "You're pouty" or "You're pushy." Finally, I showed it to Mom.

"He says you're pretty," she said. "Isn't that sweet?"

17

MOM STOPPED laying down the silverware, as if a light bulb had popped on over her head. "How about Y camp?"

It was only the first Saturday of summer vacation, but her mind had been busy with what I was going to do with All My Free Time. She began to study me, as if with just a little water, I could start blooming daisies straight out of my head. Enrichment, she said, I needed some *enrichment*.

"I'm too old for camp," I said. "Besides, they nearly drowned me in Oregon!"

"Drowned you?"

"Yeah! *You* remember."

"I remember nothing of the kind! I was right there, Cory. You choked on some water, that's all."

"I can't believe you! It was only the worst thing that ever happened to me."

"But it didn't happen," she insisted.

I pouted for a while. She was right, I didn't almost drown. It was all the work of my overactive imagination.

"I just want to waitress," I said for the nth time. "I'll work for tips, like now."

"You're too young to work," she said. "You need sunshine, fresh air . . ."

"Well, then," I mumbled, "you should have put the restaurant in Santa Catarina where the beach is."

Mom's eyes teared up. She held the bunch of silver to her chest, like a bouquet.

"*What?* What did I say?"

"Nothing. I was just thinking about your father."

And then I felt bad. We hadn't had a real argument since Sonny left. It was like living in a truce, and I didn't want to break it.

We finished setting out the silver and the paper napkins. You couldn't do sailboats with paper napkins, but it was a cheaper way to go.

"Sam asked me to marry him," Mom said, just like that. She said it to the travel poster of Ireland, like a sleepwalker.

"*What?*"

She turned her head, a gentle, funny look in her eyes. "Don't be mad," she said. "Sam's very sweet."

The air whooshed out of me. I slid out a chair and dropped into it. "How come he asked you to marry him? I didn't think you were even dating."

"Well, *he* did, I guess."

"I don't understand," I said in my ten-year-old voice, which I thought was gone for good.

Mom sat across from me. She laid her hand on my arm and looked me straight in the eye. She had the prettiest gray eyes, which I didn't get, mine being about as many colors as a calico cat. "Don't worry. I'm not going to marry him."

"You're not? Are you sure?"

"Sure I'm sure. I'm not in love with Sam."

"Are you sure?"

She laughed. "Sure, I'm sure."

I pushed on. "How do you *know*?"

"What? How do you know when you're not in love?"

"Yeah. How do you know that?"

Mom laid her chin on her fist. "I don't know . . ." she said. "I just don't feel any different when Sam's around. I'm always glad to see him, but he doesn't, well, he doesn't make my bells ring." She got this goofy look on her face.

"Did Dad?"

"Make my bells ring? You bet he did!"

We sat there for a while thinking about Dad. He always made you laugh, was the thing. And he had that Sonny way of looking at you, as if he had all the time in the world for whatever dumb thing you might say.

"Do you love yourself, Mom?"

"Do I love myself?" That stopped her for a minute. What

Lawrence had said in his van that night was like a puzzle to me. It sounded like a thing a person ought to do, but then again it sounded kind of selfish. Weren't we supposed to love others? Wasn't that the Golden Rule?

"Love myself? Well, I suppose I do. Well, yes, of course. Don't you? You do, don't you?" In another minute, she'd put her hand on my forehead to take my temperature.

"I guess I do. But what does it mean?" I pressed on, like a dogsled team through a storm. "Does it mean you have to love everything about you? Do you have to love the way you look?"

Mom thought about that. "Not all the time."

"Do you ever, just like, you know, look in the mirror and hate your face? I do." My tears were ready to spill, don't ask me why. It was just my mom.

"Oh, Cory, sweetie." She squeezed my arm, her face all crumpled like tissue.

"So does that mean I don't love myself?"

"No, oh *no*. That's the way teenagers are. You outgrow that," she hesitated, "*most* of it. Anyway, loving yourself is much more. More than how you look. It's, well, it's how you are inside. Respecting yourself. Being a good person."

Being a good person. There it was again. I felt like spilling the beans right then, telling her all about Lawrence and the fire. It felt like in a million years I wasn't going to be able to understand who Lawrence really was, and how a person with all that gentleness and love could do such a bad thing.

Sonny would know. Sonny could make sense of anything. Maybe it had to do with the way he put cars together, the way the pieces fit one way and one way only.

"I hope we get a letter from Sonny today," I said.

Mom was still lost in her thoughts.

I told her I'd do the Specials. It was just a blackboard hung by the front door, but it had been my idea and so I took it seriously. I wrote the Specials in several chalk colors and drew some little thing on the bottom, like a flower or a squirrel. But nothing could sell those croquettes with the mint sauce, and Mom finally gave up on them.

"I hope Sonny does something with his life," Mom said.

"He is doing something with his life," I said, but I knew what she meant.

"After the Army," she said. "Once he's discharged."

"He'll do something."

"I mean, besides working at the Esso."

I thought about what Sonny said about Dad the night of the race. "Maybe you shouldn't say anything to Sonny for a while about, you know, doing something with his life."

"Oh, well, I won't. He'll be on vacation, kind of, won't he? That's what leave is. I won't bug him." She frowned a little. "Still, there's all this stuff that needs doing around here. Sonny's so good with this old plumbing."

"Sonny didn't think Dad was very proud of him."

Her eyebrows went up in two perfect arches. "Dad? Not

proud of Sonny? Why ever would he think a thing like that? Dad was so proud of both of you!"

"Well, Sonny didn't think so."

"Oh, dear," she said.

"You're not going to cry, are you? Because if you are, I'm not going to tell you everything." I think she knew I didn't tell her everything. She wasn't dumb.

"I'm not going to cry. It takes too long to put on my makeup. It just makes me feel sad, that's all."

"Well, I told Sonny he was wrong."

"Good. Good for you." She looked like she was smiling away the rain. "Won't it be great to have Sonny home again?" She tucked some of my loose hair behind my ear. "I like those new glasses," she said. "They give you a softer look, more feminine."

She didn't know unisex was in. There was so much she didn't know, but she tried hard. Some mothers didn't try at all. Like Lisa's mother, who still wore her hair like Lucy Ricardo.

When Mom finally realized Dad's glasses weren't around anymore, I told her they'd slid off my nose and broken. She said, no wonder. They weren't meant for my face. If you went through life wearing somebody else's glasses, she said, you were bound to get a "distorted view of things."

"Wait till Sonny sees how much you've grown in one year. He won't believe it."

I pictured Sonny bursting through the door and grabbing

us both in a bear hug. I didn't care if he went back to working at the Esso after he was finished with the Army. Things would be normal again, if he did. He'd race the Ford at the drags. We'd cruise like before. I could ask him all the dumb questions that were clogging up my life. Sonny was a good mechanic. There was nothing wrong with working at the Esso.

"I'll cross off today," I said, jumping up. "That'll make just thirty-eight days to go." The Ojala Pharmacy calendar with all the months of red X's hung over Mom's prep table. June had a special on hemorrhoid cream, two for the price of one.

"No!" she said. "Don't do that!"

"Why?"

"It's bad luck," she said. "The day isn't over yet."

We waited almost three weeks for Sonny's next letter. It didn't say much, except what Sonny always said at the end, which was to take care of ourselves. He'd be home on the sixth of August. No exclamation points. No can't-wait-to-get-home. Just the date. On the calendar, I drew a big red heart around it.

"The shorter the time gets, the more nervous I get," said Mom. "I know that's superstition. I know he's fine. I *know* that." But she didn't look convinced.

18

MOM GAVE ME three lunches to work, Thursday through Saturday, and wrote me on the schedule like a regular person. This was on the condition that I get out into the fresh air on the other four days.

Lisa called on Monday. She and Jimbo had broken up again. She didn't cry about it the way she once did, and use up all our girl time. "Come for lunch," I said, which is what grownup women friends said on the down times.

"How do I get there?"

"What do you mean? You go down Signal to Matilija—"

"I know where you live, dummy. Jimbo's only dropped me off there a hundred times. But, you know, how do I *get* there?"

I couldn't believe this was so hard for her. "You walk," I said. "You know, you move those things on the ends of your legs."

"Walk? All the way from my house to the café?"

"Lisa, it's six blocks."

It took some coaxing, but she finally gave in. I reserved us the window table and Patsy waited on us as if we were perfect strangers.

Of course, we had to yak about Jimbo first. Lisa talked about him the way you talk about a job you're tired of.

"I know what's wrong," I said. "Jimbo doesn't ring your bells anymore."

Lisa's milk shot straight out of her mouth and down the front of her tie-dyed T-shirt. She jumped up, brushing off the milk while I pounded her on the back. We got a lot of dirty looks from other customers before we were through.

"Ring my bells?" Lisa busted up. "That's the funniest thing I ever heard!" After a while, she calmed down. I was feeling a little sorry for Mom right then, to tell you the truth. Then Lisa said, biting her cheek, which she did in deep thought, "It's sort of true, I guess, the bells thing. All we do is sit around and watch TV. And then he wants to do, you know, *that*. Which is boring."

"Boring?"

"Yeah," she sighed, like somebody about thirty years old. "Boring."

"Doing it is *boring*?" I could hardly believe my ears.

Lisa gave me the big sister look, which I hate. Just because I was not experienced in the sex department, like she was.

Sex was a catch-22. You couldn't really know about sex without doing it, but how could you do it if you didn't know how?

"Take my word," she said. "With Jimbo, it's boring."

Of course, I couldn't say who besides her would ever want to do it with Jimbo in the first place.

Lisa licked mayonnaise off her fingers. "Guess who I saw the other day?"

"Who?"

"Lawrence."

My heart jumped out of my throat and sat there on the table, panting like a dog. "Lawrence?" I said weakly.

"Well, his van. I don't think it was him driving it though."

"Who? Who was driving it?"

"I dunno." She shrugged. "Did I tell you that Jimbo's going to—"

"I mean, was it a guy?"

Lisa groaned. "Get over it, Cory! Lawrence is too old for you."

"But you're the one who said he wasn't!" I felt like biting her. "And anyway, I *am* over it."

And then, as her eyes got wider and wider, I broke down and told her everything.

"Oh, my God," she said, her hand on her throat. "Let's get out of here."

I left Patsy a big fat tip, and we headed downtown.

"I can't believe you were actually there!" Lisa had to stop every couple of minutes to tie her sandal laces. My tennies weren't exactly cool, but at least they could walk. "It was on the national news and everything. Governor Reagan even came to the university, did you know that? He's so handsome."

"Well, he's a movie star. He's supposed to be handsome."

"There's a reward out, you know. Ten thousand bucks!"

"I know."

Here, I would like to say that I didn't spend that money about a hundred ways, taking a vacation to Hollywood and of course buying Dad's stone, the most expensive one. I would like to *say* it, but it wouldn't be true.

"Well, go for it!"

"What? Turn Lawrence in?" Jason drove by with a carload of guys. They honked and yelled obscene things, as usual. Lisa flipped them off.

"Sure." She shrugged.

"I can't believe you can say that. After all he did."

"What? Run the debate team?"

"No. Not just that. He"—it was hard to put in words— "he raised our consciousness!"

"Oh, Cory. He was just turning us into draft dodgers like him. A history teacher isn't supposed to tell you what you should think. That's brainwashing."

"I told him I loved him," I said miserably. We were crossing to the Frostee. Lisa said Jimbo was the last person she wanted to see, but you'd have to be missing some spark plugs to believe that.

"You did *what?*" She stopped, right square in the middle of the street and I had to lead her across like a blind person. "What did he say?"

"He said I should love myself."

"What a creep!" she said.

We got our Frostees and went to sit down. Lisa kept turning around, pretending she was brushing something off her shoulder, but I knew she was looking for Jimbo.

Jason drove in and parked in his spot. The guys got out acting tough, spitting, lighting up. They were all still in high school. Every one of them wanted to be Jason. He was 4F because of a trick knee, but that didn't seem to matter. He did just the one thing on New Year's Eve and, for that, he was famous.

Jason strolled over, his thumbs hooked in his pockets. He still wore his hair the old way, with the little curl over his forehead, like Kookie in the fifties. Mom said Jason was just a big fish in a little pond.

"Jimbo's looking for you, Lisa."

"So?"

Jason sat on the table, brushing something invisible off his chinos that looked brand-new. A pack of Larks was rolled into the sleeve of his white T-shirt. You could just make out the name through the fabric.

He turned his attention to me. "I hear Sonny's coming home on leave."

If you aren't a good swimmer, even a small fish can make you nervous.

"Not till August," I said.

"We'll throw him a party." And then, almost as if he was talking about cleaning up trash or doing some other dumb job, he said, "And we'll have to do Carne again." He sighed, frowning down at his hands.

"Why?"

"Why? *Why?*" He shook his head sadly. If I didn't know, well, then what was the world coming to? "Ask Sonny. He'll tell you." Jason squinted, trying to wriggle his mind into mine. "You think he won't race me? You think Sonny's a chicken?"

"Of course he's going to race you," I said hotly. "You know Sonny's not a chicken."

"Why? Because he's this big soldier?"

"Sonny's not a chicken," I repeated. "You know that."

Then Lisa changed the subject. She was going to be a bridesmaid in Jason and Sheila's wedding, but Sheila hadn't decided on the colors.

Jason pulled a toothpick out of his pocket and began cleaning his already clean fingernails. "I think she said orange."

"Orange!" cried Lisa, horrified. "We'll all look like pumpkins."

19

LISA WAS ON THE TABLE in the middle of the dining room. I was pinning up her hem inch by inch, trying not to stick my fingers and bleed all over her bridesmaid's dress. It was the kind of dress that made you glad you weren't in the wedding, with big orange doohickeys stuck to both shoulders. Lisa said they were roses, but they looked more like cabbages, giant orange cabbages.

Mom came in from the kitchen where she was getting ready to wash the floor. Her head was done up like Aunt Jemima.

"That dress is perfect for you, Lisa," she said. "It's not orange. It's . . . tangerine. Or, I know! orange sherbet. It's very flattering in the bust."

Lisa said thank you, very sweetly, but she rolled her eyes the minute Mom's back was turned.

Lisa was back with Jimbo. He'd dropped her off, but there he was out the window every ten minutes, passing the café on his way to the bowling alley and back to the turnaround tree.

"I thought you were bored," I said, poking a pin through two stiff layers of taffeta.

"I am."

"I don't get it."

"What's there to get?" She shrugged and popped her gum.

There was a knock on the door, even though the sign said CLOSED TUESDAY.

"Get the door, will you Cory?" Mom yelled from the kitchen. "I've washed myself into a corner."

I set down the pincushion and went to the door. "We're closed," I said, even before I opened it.

"Telegram," said the kid on the bike. "Sign here."

I blinked. I could smell the kid's sweat. There was sweat on the pen that he handed me. I scribbled my name. He gave me a skinny yellow envelope. I yelled for Mom. The sky was so blue. It was like it was trying to keep your mind away from what was in your hand.

WESTERN UNION TELEGRAM

SY WAO34CBVT GOVT PDB=

WASHINGTON DC 8 955P EST=

MRS SPENCER DAVIES, DO NOT DLR BTWN

10PM AND 6AM LOCAL TIME DO NOT PHONE

CHECK DLY CHGS ABOVE 75CTS=

750 OJALA AVE OJALA CA

REPORT OF INJURY: THIS IS TO INFORM YOU

THAT YOUR SON PRIVATE FIRST CLASS BRIAN E

DAVIES WAS INJURED JUNE 17 1968 IN QUANG TRI PROVINCE, REPUBLIC OF VIETNAM. HE SUSTAINED A WOUND TO THE LEFT FLANK WHILE ON OPERATION. HE WAS TREATED IN THE FIELD. HIS CONDITION AND PROGNOSIS ARE EXCELLENT. IT IS HOPED THAT HE WILL COMMUNICATE WITH YOU SOON INFORMING YOU OF HIS WELFARE. HERBERT T WILSON USARMY LTGEN

"Oh, my God," said Mom, the telegram shaking in her hands. "Oh, my God. Sonny."

"Come inside, Mrs. Davies," said Lisa. "Cory, get your mom a shot of something. I think she's gonna faint."

"No, no, I'm fine." Mom folded the telegram and slid it back in its envelope. She closed the door carefully, both hands pressing. Then she laid her forehead against it and closed her eyes.

"It's just a flesh wound," I said. "It's just a flesh wound." Once you heard that line in a movie, you knew everything was all right. But it didn't work that way in real life. In real life, it just sounded like a movie line.

"All day yesterday, I knew something was going to happen," Mom said. "I didn't want to think that way, but I couldn't help it. I just had this . . . this feeling of dread."

She went to the window and stared out, just as Jimbo sailed

by in his pickup. "There's Jimbo," she said, and then she started to cry.

"Can I get you anything?" Lisa said. "A cup of tea?"

Mom blew her nose in a napkin and stuffed the napkin in her pocket. "That's a good idea, Lisa," she said. "Thank you."

Lisa headed for the kitchen. I followed her.

"That's okay," I said, as Lisa put the kettle on the stove. "I'll do it."

"Are you sure?"

"Sure," I said.

Lisa turned and put her arms around me. She didn't stick her butt out like some girls do, and she didn't pat me on the back like a baby. She just let me hold on to her until I was finished soaking the front of her bridesmaid's dress.

"Sonny's okay," she said. "Sonny's okay. It's over. The thing you were worried about. It's over. Sonny's okay now."

———————

June 29, 1968

Dear Mom and Sis,

By now you have heard about me getting wounded. I know you guys are worried, but it wasn't much, honest. I'll be back on two feet in a couple of days. They say I could get a medical discharge, but I've seen guys with worse who are still here. I got the Purple Heart, but it's not for being a hero or anything. I didn't even know what was happening until it was over. Could have been worse. Lost two buddies in three weeks. One of them was in the picture I sent. His name was Billy Bo. I helped carry him out and it was bad. I don't mind saying I cried like a baby after. Now I keep thinking about him like this bad dream that goes on and on, I guess because I was there and saw it happen. War is like that I guess. They say you get used to it, but I don't know. Best not to get too attached to anybody. One minute they're fine, and the next minute they're not. I think about Dad a lot, how quick he was gone. Sorry for being so down. Sometimes I don't know if I can be the same person after this. I have seen too much of the dark side of things. But the main thing is to make it out of here, right? Don't think I have forgotten that your birthday is coming up, Cory. Wish I could be there. I can't believe my little sis will be driving soon. Take care, you two. Love, Sonny

---

Mom asked me if I wanted my birthday off, but I said I'd work. It felt like any other day. I kept waiting for fifteen to kick in, a sign or something. I looked in the mirror, first thing. I still looked fourteen, even though I'd gone from a 30AA bra to a 32B, all in one year.

Thursday lunches were slow, so I usually worked them myself. That way I got to keep all the tips. Sam came in with Maria, then Patsy and Karen. They sat down like regular customers, expecting to be waited on, and soon the dining room was full.

All of a sudden, out came Mom, carrying a birthday cake, blazing with candles. You think fifteen's not much till you see all the candles. Maria stood, and then everybody in the whole dining room stood up as if I were a somebody. "Happy birthday, dear Co-ry," sang everybody (except for the ones who sang "Happy birthday, dear hum-n-hum," because they didn't know my name). My face was so hot, I thought I might blow up. But it felt like my birthday after that. Mom gave me a beautiful silver chain bracelet, with a silver 15 charm on it. Also got: pearl earrings, a book of poetry by Edna St. Vincent Millay, Arlo Guthrie's latest, and *The Facts of Life and Love for Teenagers.* The sex book was from Lisa, along with Pink Passion nail polish, which is prettier in the bottle than on your toenails.

The next morning, Lisa called from the pharmacy. I could tell where she was because of the bells on the door whenever anybody went in or out. "Cory!" She sounded out of breath. "Did you do it? Were you the one?"

"The one what?"

"The one who turned him in! Lawrence! It's in the papers." I heard a rustle of newspaper and Jimbo yelling for her to hurry up.

"He got caught? Lawrence is in jail?"

"Yeah!" Her hand muffled the phone, but I heard her yell back plain as day, "Don't you dare leave! Can't you see this is important?

"So it wasn't you? You didn't get the reward?" she breathed back into the phone.

"Of course not!" My heart nearly stopped. "Oh, my god, Lisa. What if he thinks it *was* me?"

"But you said he didn't see you."

"I don't know if he saw me or not. He just didn't *act* like he saw me. But what if he did?"

"He would have said something if he saw you, Cory."

"How do you know?"

"Lawrence? Ha! He'd have made some big history lesson out of it."

"Lisa?"

"Yeah?"

"You think Jimbo did it?"

The air went dead for a minute.

"You told him, didn't you?"

"Well, yeah, but I told him not to tell."

We got our first telephone call from Sonny that night. It lasted about five minutes, Sonny having to remind us every minute to say "Over" when we were done talking. He was fine, he said. He was sorry to worry us by getting shot. He wouldn't be able to write for a while because they were going "up country," but he didn't want us to worry about that either. Sometimes it was hard to write anyway, he said, because there was no good stuff to write about. Over.

Mom tried to tell him he could write about anything, just write. But she forgot to say "Over," so Sonny was talking to her at the same time she was trying to talk to him. Plus Mom and I both had our ears on the receiver and were talking at the same time, which didn't help. *We love you!* we both yelled as if he was halfway around the world, which he was, but by then he was gone.

―――――――

Lawrence was on the front of the *Los Angeles Times* and the *New York Times* and on the inside of a bunch more papers. The library had them all. His hands were cuffed behind him. He was hunched forward, his hair was longer and hanging past his face. "Philanthropist's Son Arrested," said the headline. My eyes skimmed the story faster than my mind could follow:

Marion Taylor Lawrence III, son and heir to the Lawrence Mining Company fortune, was arrested in Berkeley, California, and charged in connection with the burning of the United States Army Recruiting Center, near the University of California, Santa Catarina. He was released to the custody of his father, Marion Taylor Lawrence II, of San Francisco. The amount of bail was undisclosed. Arraignment is set for the end of September.

Marion? Lawrence's real name was Marion?

I bought a copy of the *Los Angeles Times* at the pharmacy, remembering how it was Lawrence who made us read that paper in the first place. When I got home, I took it upstairs and spread it out on my bed. I stared at the picture of Lawrence for the longest time, and then I cut it out. What if he'd been caught because of me? Because of my big fat mouth?

I pulled the phone on its extra long cord from Mom's side

of the room to mine. I put the phone on my bed and dialed San Francisco information. No one by the name of Marion Taylor Lawrence was listed, I guess because they were rich.

Then I dialed the number of the Ojala School District, which was two rooms attached to the post office. "I'm calling about one of your employees," I said, pinching my nose.

"Yes."

"A . . . let's see here . . . a Marion Taylor Lawrence."

"Who is this?"

"FBI," I said. "Special Investigator Maria . . . Puccini. We need to verify a telephone number."

"For a Mrs. Lawrence you said?"

"*Mister* Lawrence."

"Just a moment, please." I heard the phone being laid down and the click of high heels.

I relaxed my stranglehold on the receiver and wiped the sweat off my face. I heard a file cabinet open, then close. A rustle of papers.

"The permanent telephone number we have for this employee is 415-555-7771. Is that what you have?"

"Yes," I said, so excited I could barely scribble the number. "That's it. Thanks!"

I hung up the phone and yelped.

"Cory? What's wrong?" Mom called up the stairs.

"Nothing! Nothing's wrong. I bit my finger."

"You what?"

"Never mind."

I dialed Lawrence's number. It rang twenty-seven times. No answer. I stuck his number under my pillow and went downstairs.

Mom was mixing egg yolk and catsup into a meat loaf with her hands. "Do you think Sonny will want a party?" she said. "Some kind of celebration?"

The calendar was marked down to twenty-two days. Mom wasn't sleeping well. There were dark shadows under her eyes. She'd outgrown the Cher thing. Now she wore no makeup at all, which made her look like she was just getting out of bed all day long.

Sam told her she was working too hard, that she needed more help. All she needed was for Sonny to come home in one piece, she said.

"Sonny isn't a party kind of guy." I was thinking how the kids would throw him one anyway, and how that was the best way to be welcomed back home, with a bonfire big as Saint Thomas Aquinas.

"Well, what should we do? Just go pick him up at the airport?"

"Sure. I guess."

"Just the two of us? Maybe he'd like to see some of his friends." She frowned. "You know, in the old days there were big parades when our soldiers came home. Now everybody acts like they're something to be ashamed of."

In the paper were these horrible pictures of death and destruction, of little children running and screaming in fear. People didn't want that kind of war. They wanted the kind you saw in the movies, where the soldiers wore starched uniforms with ironed creases in their pants and they all had medals for bravery.

"Look at this," she said, turning the cookbook so that I could read what was scribbled down the margin: "Sonny's birthday meatloaf. Age 14. Extra onion and dried mustard. Sonny's a good strong boy, and we are prou—". The rest was smeared with catsup.

"It was right here between the meat loaf page and the roast beef," Mom said. "See? I told you Dad was proud of Sonny."

I waited until I heard Mom doing her little snuffle snores, which told me she was sound asleep, at least for the time being. Then I crept downstairs. Feckless followed me down, her nails clicking behind. The kitchen was filled with moon shadows, making everything look bigger than it was and kind of spooky. Feckless pushed her doggie bowl around with her nose. I made sure the back door was locked. Then I sat on the prep table with the phone in my lap and dialed the number from memory.

It was 405 miles from Ojala to San Francisco, not so far. You could drive it in about six hours. But the ring of the phone sounded far away, like it was coming from China. My stomach was tied in knots and wouldn't let go.

"Hello?"

His voice was exactly the same. Tears stung my eyes.

"Lawrence?"

"Who is this?"

"It's Cory. Corin Davies. Remember?"

"Corin!" The same laugh, like a warm breeze through an open window. "Of course I remember. How are you, Corin?"

"Um, fine. How are you?"

"Corin." Softly this time. "I'm sorry I didn't get a chance to say goodbye to you, you and all the other kids."

"That's okay."

"How are you doing? How's Sonny?" Sonny. He remembered Sonny's name.

I told him about Sonny getting shot and how he was coming home in a couple of weeks. Lawrence said that was good.

I told him there was a chance Sonny would get a medical discharge.

Lawrence said that was great.

Then his voice changed, and a chill ran through me. "How did you get this number?"

But he laughed when I told him about Maria Puccini, the FBI agent.

We didn't say anything for a little bit, then we both started up at once. I let him go first.

"Corin, what the paper said . . ." He stopped.

"Yes?"

"Well, you can't believe everything you read. You know that

by now, right? Some janitor turned me in. Said he ran out the back of the building just before it went up and saw me pushing the dumpster. It was a case of mistaken identity, that's all."

I don't know why I had to make him say it, but I did. I'd seen him with my own two eyes, with my glasses on. I wouldn't have mistaken Lawrence for anybody. "You really didn't do it then? You didn't burn that building?"

"Of course not! Oh, Corin, I thought you of all people would know I couldn't do a thing like that. They got the wrong guy! I wasn't anywhere near the U that night."

"Oh."

When a heart shrivels up, it's like making a fist. It doesn't want to open for a while after that.

Lawrence went on, saying how his father had gotten together a whole team of expensive lawyers. His hair was short now, what did I think about that? Cold ears. He said something about cold ears, but I wasn't listening anymore.

"Well, I've got to go now," I said.

"Oh, well, sure." He had more to say, I guess, but I didn't. "Well, thanks for calling, Corin. And keep that debate team going, okay? You can do it."

I set the receiver down and watched the sweat dry off. It didn't take as long as you'd think.

20

"SINCE WHEN ARE YOU SMOKING?"

Mom nearly jumped out of her nightgown. I'd caught her at her window, staring out, blowing clouds into the dark. "Cory! I thought you were asleep. I'm *not*. I mean, I'm not exactly starting a *habit* or anything. It calms my nerves, that's all."

"I thought it was Dad," I said, my tongue still thick with sleep. "I woke up and I thought I smelled Dad."

She touched my hair. "Go back to bed," she said. "I'll put this thing out."

The hot winds were back, just like the year before. They made you anxious, even if you didn't have anything to be anxious about, which we did, and so it was hard to sleep.

"Are you worried about Sonny?" I asked, a dumb question.

She rubbed her arms as if they were cold. "A little."

"Are you getting one of your feelings? Is something wrong? Has something happened to Sonny?"

In Sonny's last letter he'd said his wound wasn't healing as it should. An infection had set in. He'd been back to see the medics a couple of times. They told him it was the climate and gave him stuff to put on it. It was all they could do.

"No. No, I don't think anything's happened," Mom said. "Really, I don't. It's just that with so little time left . . ."

"Superstition. You said it yourself."

"You're right. You are absolutely right."

But she didn't sleep much the next night, or the night after that. I know, because I didn't either. On August 5th we never went to bed at all. As the hands on the teapot clock met at midnight in the ghostly fluorescent light of the kitchen we toasted Sonny with glasses of cold milk. It was hot as daytime, almost. We laid butcher paper across the dining room floor and painted a banner. SONNY'S DAY. WELCOME HOME, SONNY!!! CAFÉ CLOSED. At dawn, we were hanging it above the front door, over the Ojala Café sign.

"I still think we should hire a band or something," said Mom, squinting up at the bright blue letters on the banner. "Couldn't you get the school band?"

I just stared at her until she got it. I didn't know one person in the school band. I didn't even know if they practiced in the summer. By the sound of them, they didn't practice at all.

"Well, we'd better get on the road," she said. After Mom's sleepless nights, her eyes looked like the bride of Frankenstein.

"Mother, it's six o'clock in the morning."

"We don't want Sonny to get there before us!" She folded

the ladder and we carried it to the garage. "What would he think if we weren't there to meet him?"

I opened the garage door. She dragged the ladder inside. The Ford with all its secrets sat there gleaming in the dark.

"We'll be two hours early," I said, "even as slow as you drive."

"I don't want to argue. Just go and get ready." She laid the ladder against the wall. "Besides, now that you have your learner's permit, you can drive."

"Then let's take Sonny's car."

Mom looked at the Ford as if it had fangs. "Well," she said uncertainly, "if you think you can drive it . . ."

The telephone rang. My heart grabbed. *The plane went down. Sonny never got to the plane at all. The Army was keeping him another year.* Mom made a dash inside.

"It was just Sam," she said, relieved. She didn't trust the telephone any more than I did, not since Dad. "He offered to drive us, but I said you wanted to."

Mom and Sam weren't dating. It was worse than that. He hung out. From upstairs, I'd hear the quiet hum of their voices, hers high, his deep, for hours after the café had closed. At fourteen, you could creep down the stairs and eavesdrop, but according to *The Facts of Life and Love for Teenagers*, fifteen was supposed to have more dignity. Besides, at fifteen, there are things you'd rather not hear until you absolutely have to. Fifteen was more sophisticated than fourteen, but it wasn't nearly as brave.

I went up to get ready. In no time, my bed was piled with clothes. Everything made me look babyish, or fat, or like a hippie. Mom was ready in a flash. "Hurry!" she called, tripping lightly down the stairs.

I pulled a neon-yellow-and-green dress over my head and tore it right off. "Yuck!" Then came a new pair of bell-bottoms (too tight), and finally a peasant blouse and cut-off jeans miniskirt.

The Ford horn blared. "Cory! Come on!" I took one last look in the mirror, trying to imagine how I would look to Sonny after all this time. Making a ponytail out of my hair was like tying a ribbon around Brillo. I mean, what was the use? But leaving it down made me look like Jerry Garcia, not exactly a Sonny favorite. Besides, in the heat, a ponytail was cooler.

I crisscrossed my new sandals up to my knees and clumped down the stairs.

"It's about time!" Mom said, as I slid behind the wheel. "Aren't you going to wear your pearl earrings?"

"Nuh-uh." The earrings Sam had given me for my birthday were probably real, but *pearls*? Pearls were so uncool. Of course, Sam couldn't know that. He was over fifty years old.

"How come?"

"Too hot."

I slung my arm over the seat and, without a second thought, backed Sonny's car onto the street. Sparks of sunlight shot off the hood. There were three coats of wax on that hood. I knew Sonny would appreciate that. I shifted into low.

Mom's eyes followed my hands. "When did you learn to do that?"

"What?"

"Shift the gears."

"Huh?" Stalling.

"I thought you only knew automatic."

I shrugged. "I dunno. It's pretty much the same." I counted on Mom's not knowing, being she was an automatic person herself. "You should try it."

"Oh, no," she said, waving the idea away. "It's hard enough as it is."

We were halfway there before I realized a terrible thing: Mom and I were wearing the exact same outfit, jeans miniskirts and white peasant blouses. Except for our hair—my frizz ball versus her shag—we looked the same. It was creepy. It was so *wrong!* I almost turned the Ford around so I could go home and change. How could I not have noticed before? On the way to the airport with Sonny one year ago, Mom had worn her pink-and-white-striped shirtwaist dress and pumps. She looked like a PTA mom, which is what she was supposed to be.

"Move over," I said. Mom had this way of sitting in the middle of her side.

She didn't move. "Why?"

"That's where you're supposed to sit. By the door."

"Who says?"

Did I have to explain *everything* to her? "Mother, people will think we're, you know . . ."

"What? What will they think, Cory?"

"That we're lezzies!"

"Who will think we're lesbians, Cory?" She said this slowly and carefully, the way you talk to lunatics.

"People!"

"What people?"

"People!" I practically shrieked. I was beginning to think she was never going to get all the things you're supposed to get, especially by her age. But she was laughing so hard, I don't think she even cared.

The ocean went by like it does, as if it's going to be around forever and you're not.

"Look, Cory, pelicans!" Mom's arm shot past my nose. I swerved into the fast lane, where nobody happened to be. A long line of pelicans dipped and sailed over the waves, playing follow the leader.

We didn't talk much after that, which made my driving better.

How would it be with Sonny home? I'd worried so much about getting him here, there wasn't much worry left over for anything else. Mom and I had somehow made a life without him, without Dad. Just the two of us. There were lots of lonely times and I knew there still would be. There was no getting over Dad. There was the going on from day to day, that's all. But we'd learned to do that, Mom and me.

It wasn't so hard to figure out how to let somebody go. You

took one step, you breathed one breath, and then you did that all over again. You breathed, and you took the next step, and then, one day, you didn't even know why, you heard yourself laughing. You didn't want to laugh. It felt wrong to laugh when somebody you loved was gone. But you had to, just like you had to breathe.

It wasn't so hard to figure out this stuff, it was just hard to do it.

I turned onto the airport road, slowing and shifting down. "I just can't get over how well you drive," Mom said. "Sonny is going to be so surprised." She stuck her head out the window as a small plane buzzed over. "Do you think that's his plane? I'll bet that's his plane!"

It wasn't Sonny's plane. Sonny's plane wasn't due for two hours and fifteen minutes. We parked in the lot and headed for the terminal. "I told you we'd be early," I said, stopping a couple of times to retie my sandals.

Mom popped a magazine out of her fishnet bag, found a bench to sit on, and started flipping through the pages, which left me wandering around reading timetables and looking for cute mechanics.

I kept thinking about Luis's family, crying and hugging him, carrying him to the gate. The hardest thing I ever had to write in a letter to Sonny was that Luis didn't make it. Then came one of those times when Sonny didn't write. Finally, we heard from him. I read the letter twice. Not a word about Luis.

That's when I began to think that Sonny wasn't getting all his letters, that some of them got lost or shot down or something. It wasn't like Sonny not to say one thing about Luis.

Now I was going to have to tell him in person, which was harder. I'd try to do better than I did telling Sonny about Dad, now that I had some experience, but this wasn't exactly the kind of thing a person wanted to get real good at: Professional Bad-News Giver.

Mom was squinting into the sky instead of reading her magazine. I paced back and forth in front of her bench and ate a 3 Musketeers bar practically whole.

Time went by like it was clogged in a drain.

"That's it!" cried Mom, after what seemed like a day and a half. "That's got to be him." A blue commuter plane was dropping down for a landing. Mom stuffed her magazine into her bag and took off. I was right behind her. Through the chain-link fence, we watched the plane taxi down the runway and stop. The engine shuddered and went dead. The propellers slowed. The propellers stopped. Nothing happened for about five minutes. Then the door finally opened and the steps dropped down. Mom was clinging to the fence like a prisoner. My heart was beating something crazy.

Out came a businessman in a brown suit, then a woman with a baby slung over her shoulder like laundry, a grandma, another businessman, two blond-headed kids who were maybe twins. Then nobody.

"There he is!" cried Mom. "Sonny! Sonny!" She waved her arms frantically. Sonny came down the steps looking like the day he left, blue shirt and all. Right then, for just those few minutes, I wanted to be fourteen again. I wanted to jump up and down shrieking Sonny's name, but of course I couldn't.

They opened the gate and the passengers crowded through. Sonny waited at the back. He was frowning, looking way out past the airport, thinking I couldn't tell what.

"Sonny!" Mom cried again. This time, he heard. His face lit up. People streamed by. And then we were hugging, the three of us together in a puppy swarm, so many tears you couldn't tell whose were whose.

"I can't believe you're here," Mom said over and over, holding Sonny at arm's length, giving him a shake. Sonny's hair was long. It kept falling in his face. He'd push it back or jerk his head, but it fell right back. His eyes were bloodshot and he needed a shave, but nobody had ever looked so good to me as Sonny did right then.

"How's your leg, Sonny?" Mom asked, which was when I first realized that he'd limped down the steps from the plane.

He stared at Mom in the strangest way. "What's this getup? Are you wearing Cory's stuff now?"

"Oh!" Mom's face turned pink. "Isn't it funny? I didn't know we were wearing the same outfit until we were almost here!"

I knew what was going through Sonny's mind. He was looking for the shirtwaist Mom, but the only thing left of her was the tiny gold locket from Dad. It winked from a chain around her neck.

"Well!" said Mom, clapping her hands like a magician. "Guess who drove us here? And guess whose car she drove?"

Sonny shot me his old grin. I felt suddenly shy, I don't know why.

Mom and Sonny walked arm in arm, Sonny limping just a little. I walked behind them, carrying Sonny's duffel. Mom's legs were good for forty. She looked from the back as if she could be his girlfriend.

When we got to the car, Sonny laid his hand on the hood. A corner of his mouth crept up, but he didn't say anything. He didn't say how good the Ford looked, but I could tell he was thinking it.

I held out the keys.

Sonny took them. "Don't you want to drive?"

"I don't care," I said.

He slid into the driver's seat and started her up. It was strange how different she sounded. Sweeter. Smoother. If a car can wait, that Ford had surely been waiting for Sonny.

Coming back into town, I noticed things I hadn't thought much about before. Like the flag flying upside down at a house down the street. When Sonny left there were lots of flags and they all flew the way they were supposed to. A year ago the *Ojala Sun* printed the names of boys going into the service, now they printed editorials saying what a mistake Vietnam was for our country. If Sonny noticed the upside-down flag, he didn't say anything about it. But then he wasn't saying much.

At home, Sonny went straight inside without looking up at the banner, but I figured he had to have seen his name in bright blue twelve-inch letters. He glanced around the dining room, just like that woman in the droopy feathered hat. "It looks different," he said. "What did you do to it?"

Feckless was whining and scraping at the back door.

"Oh!" Mom said. I could tell she was trying to see the dining room through Sonny's eyes. "Well! We changed the tablecloths to white. But that was after you were gone, wasn't it? The curtains, of course, instead of those hideous window shades . . . Oh, and the walls. They were that awful green, you remember. Off-white opens up the room, don't you think?"

But Sonny's mind was locked down on something. "Yeah, fine," he said. He stomped into the kitchen. Mom looked at me with something like panic on her face. I shrugged. Sonny came out, Feckless dancing around his legs, slathering all over him. But Sonny kept stepping around her, as if she wasn't there. At last, he reached down and patted her head without looking, missing all that love. "What happened to the stove?"

"Oh, that old thing! I gave it to the Salvation Army. Only two burners worked."

"Dad never complained about it."

"Sonny, that stove *came* from the Salvation Army. It was worn out!"

"Yeah," Sonny said, brushing the hair out of his face.

"Worn out." He laughed like a gunshot. "I'm worn out. Guess I'll go up and crash for a while."

"Don't you want something to eat? You must be starved."

"No, I'm fine." He picked up his duffel. He stood there for a minute like he was trying to come up with the right thing to say. "It's good to be home."

Mom and I listened to Sonny trudging up the stairs, heavy on the right foot. Feckless stood whining at the door that Sonny had closed behind her.

"Well," Mom said, "he's home." As if she wasn't quite sure.

I went out to the garage. I closed the door very quietly behind me. Then I got into the Ford on the driver's side. There were tiny cracks all around the wheel and on the knob of the gearshift. The mirror wouldn't stay straight no matter what you did. The leather on the seat was cracked, too, and fading to white in the places where you sat. It made me cry, all that cracking and fading. I couldn't stop crying about it.

After a while, I went back into the house. Mom was making Sonny's favorite cherry pie, crisscrossing strips of dough like she was performing major surgery. "I think he'll be just fine," she said.

"I know."

"It must be a real adjustment."

"Well, sure!"

Sonny slept through dinner. At seven, I crept up the stairs to make sure he was breathing. At nine, Mom went up. At eleven, we went to bed ourselves. Sonny was snoring softly.

Sometime in the dead of night, he yelled, "Stop!" Just that one word.

Mom called from her bed. "Sonny? You all right?"

When he didn't answer, I heard her slippered feet cross the floor. Sonny started snoring again. Mom went back to bed.

I heard her trying to wake him in the morning, heard him mumble something, but he didn't get up.

"Poor guy is exhausted," Mom said, stirring sherry into a pot of pea soup. "Patsy called. She asked if you could work lunch. I said you probably could."

"Sure."

"I'll scramble Sonny some eggs as soon as he gets up." She looked at the ceiling, then down at the soup. She needed sleep as much as Sonny did.

"Sonny's in a whole other time zone," I said.

"That's right," she said. "That's what's wrong. He's in a whole other zone."

By noon, half the tables were filled. The mayor's wife came with six of her friends. We looked at each other and thought the same thing: spaghetti. I was extra careful not to spill a crumb, but nobody ordered the spaghetti. I figured that's what they were laughing about, but you can never tell with mayors' wives.

Things were going real smooth when Sonny burst through the door. He was wearing his army pants, the camouflage kind, and no shirt at all. His chest shone with sweat.

Every head had turned and things got real quiet.

"Sonny?"

He gave me a soldier look, like I was the enemy. Then he said, "Huh!" like he'd just figured something out. He ran his hand through his shaggy hair and headed for the door. Conversation started up around me like a seized-up engine. Mom was up to her ears in chicken salad sandwiches and never heard a thing.

I was clearing the last table when she came out of the kitchen and asked if Sonny was still asleep. I told her he'd gone out. She asked where he was going. I said I didn't know.

Which is more or less the way things went. Sonny would sleep until noon, then he'd go out. Sometimes he put in some hours at the Esso, but sometimes they'd call looking for him when he said he'd be there and wasn't.

Everything was wrong, according to him. Feckless was overweight. Sam hung around too much. Didn't he have a home to go to? The café looked like some old lady's bedroom (I guess because of the lace café curtains that Mom and I both loved). Mom should be buying wholesale, not at Bayley's. She was wasting money buying at a local market. Why did she take the roast beef off the menu? It was a best-seller when Dad—

That was when Mom finally hit the roof. "I thought you repaired engines in the Army, Sonny," she said.

"Well, yeah, I did."

"You didn't cook?"

"You know I didn't cook."

"Then where is all this coming from, son? I've been cooking for a year now. On my own. Without Dad. And I've been doing just fine." She flipped open the oven door and lifted out a sizzling roasting pan. "If I need advice from my children, I'll ask for it." She set the pan on the stove like an exclamation point.

Sonny went pale. I had to feel sorry for him, even if he was being a pill. He didn't know this new Mom at all. "Don't worry," he said, "you won't get any advice from me!"

Mom reached for him. "Oh, honey, don't be like that!"

"Like *what*?"

Having Sonny gone was hard. Having him home was even harder.

His party wasn't his party at all, since he never showed up.

"What's the deal with your brother?" Jason had asked that night, his wicked little eyes narrower than ever.

I didn't have to answer. Lisa wouldn't have. But Jason always got to me. "What do you mean?"

"He's lost his edge," Jason said, "that's what's wrong. Lost his nerve."

"What's that supposed to mean?"

Lisa tried pulling me away. "Jason doesn't mean anything. He doesn't *know* what he means!"

But Sonny wasn't there at the party to defend himself. Somebody had to. "Sonny hasn't lost a thing," I said. "It's just a stupid party."

"He owes me a race, Sissy-girl," Jason said. "Sonny knows that. That's why he's not here."

"He doesn't owe you a thing."

"Oh, no? Ask him. Ask Sheila." He shot his chin over to where Sheila was laughing with a couple of her friends.

"What's it got to do with—" But Lisa gave my arm a good yank and pulled me away.

"What's that all about?"

"Sheila?"

"Yeah!"

"She spent a whole night with Sonny. You didn't know that?"

I stopped walking. "How was I supposed to know that?"

She shrugged. "I figured you knew. Everybody else did."

21

MARRYING CATSUP is one of those restaurant jobs you get when you're not so good at anything else. The problem is, nobody, I mean *nobody*, can pour catsup from one bottle into another without slopping it down the sides. It was a Tuesday, Mom was out buying vegetables. Sonny was working on the Ford. I was marrying catsup.

When the twelve bottles were filled, I mopped off the prep table and went out to the garage. The Ford's engine still dangled from the ceiling, where it had been for a week. Sonny was fiddling with something, his back to the door.

"Hi, Sonny."

He didn't turn.

"What'cha doing?" Just asking normal everyday questions made me nervous now. And being nervous around Sonny made me sad.

"Not much."

"Are you going to put the engine back?"

"Yup."

This is the way we talked now, in little sentences, pieces of thoughts.

"Sonny?"

"Mmmm?"

"Are you okay? I mean, are you all right?"

Nothing.

"Sonny?"

"I'm busy, Cory."

My throat felt like I'd swallowed glass. At fourteen, I'd have run away sobbing. But Sonny never sounded that way when I was fourteen.

"I know you're busy. I can see that."

He grabbed a rag off the bench and wiped his hands, frowning the whole time. "I'm all right. Okay?" He looked up through his hair, but I could tell it wasn't me he was seeing, not then, not the real me.

"Mom's worried."

"Well, you can tell her I'm fine. You guys hang over me like a couple of vultures! Can't you just leave a guy alone?"

We stared at each other, same Sonny, same Cory, but not the same at all. There was a space between us wider than that whole garage and I didn't know how to cross it, how to bring Sonny back.

"They missed you at the party," I said.

Sonny bit off a laugh. "I'll bet."

"Jason says you owe him a race."

Sonny reached up and slowly turned the engine, guiding it over to the Ford's open cavity.

"What should I tell him?"

"Anything you want, Cory."

"He says you've lost your nerve."

Sonny looked across the space, his eyes burning with something I'd never seen before, something dark and cold. Then he shook his head, as if Jason was a waste of words.

"Come on," he said. "I've got her back together."

It was after dark, and I'd been sitting on the porch, watching the cruisers, feeling low.

I jumped up so fast, I got dizzy. "You're taking me with you?"

"Yeah, come on."

We headed out of Ojala, the other way, toward Santa Paula, a town trying to be. The Ford purred like a spoiled cat. "She sounds great!" I said. I thought about Luis bouncing the seat, that's how excited I was. I still hadn't told Sonny about Luis. I figured somebody must have.

In the full moon, things looked stretched out, trees reaching for the few stars in a dark sky.

I watched Sonny listening to the engine. We were up to ninety in no time, shooting past what few houses there were, lit up against the night. It should have felt all right then not to talk. We were back in the space where words didn't mean as much as the thing you were supposed to feel, the power I guess it was. A hundred and ten, fifteen, smooth as those priests on wheels.

At Oak View, population 900, he let her down. We turned at El Rey del Taco, three for a buck, and headed back.

I couldn't stand it anymore. "Tell me about the war, Sonny."

His glance was like getting the skinniest piece of the cake at your own party. "Why?"

"Because I want to know. Because you used to talk to me! Just because!" Tears of frustration choked me off. I looked out into the groves, thick with night.

Sonny turned at Carne Road, the Ford's lights sweeping the trees. We drove to the end. In the moonlight you could see every chisel mark in the rock wall, every gash. Sonny said nothing. We followed a private road that wound snakelike to the top of the mountain, to a piece of flat, burnt ground where a house had been. Only the chimney was left. All of Ojala lay below us, a cluster of twinkling lights. Up here, you could forget for a little while how you made that town your whole life.

"I have to tell you something," I said.

I waited. For permission, I guess, but Sonny wasn't giving it. It was all up to me.

"I took the Ford. To a peace rally."

"Yeah?"

I shot a glance at his profile that gave nothing away now.

"I didn't have a license," I said. "I mean, I didn't even have my learner's permit. I took the *Ford!*" I said.

I remembered how it used to be, how Sonny never said anything, but that something in the air between us changed. It was how I knew he was listening.

"I had to," I said. "I had to see Lawrence."

And word after hard word, the story came tumbling out of me. Not the way I'd told it to Lisa, as if I'd been some kind of hero, but like it really was, like I really was, sick with love and fear.

Telling Sonny, I lived it all over again. Shaking inside, I finished and laid my head back against the seat.

"So that's it?" His voice was quiet, soft.

"Pretty much."

"And this Lawrence character?"

"He got arrested," I said.

Sonny nodded his head a couple of times, as if a conversation was going on inside of him that had nothing at all to do with me, or with the little world I knew.

"So why do you think he did it?" I asked. Why people did what they did was turning out to be the world's hardest question.

I thought Sonny wasn't going to answer at first. "I don't know," he said. "You get caught up in things. It feels right." His eyes seemed to beg for understanding. "It's like . . . it's like you're a part of something big, like you're *doing* something for a change. You know? Even if it turns out to be the wrong thing." He ran his fingers through his hair. "I don't know, Cory. I wish I did."

He opened the door and got out. I watched him light up a cigarette, his hands cupped against the wind. You couldn't light up like that unless you'd been doing it for a while.

And that's not all he was smoking these days. Anybody could have guessed that by looking at his eyes. Anybody but Mom.

He walked to the edge of the cliff, letting the wind tear at his clothes and his hair, standing with his feet apart and his hands behind him, cigarette burning away between his fingers. I pushed the door open and fought the wind to get to him.

Below us, the lights of Ojala caught like fish in a net.

"Remember when we used to fish, Sonny?"

"That was a long time ago," he said.

"Yeah," I sighed. "Do you wish we'd stayed in Oregon?"

"Sometimes."

"Me, too."

"Sonny——?"

"I don't want to talk about Vietnam, Cory."

"Okay."

Hot wind swirled around us, restless and unpredictable. You could hear it moaning in the distance.

"I killed people."

"Oh."

"That's what you do in the war. You kill people."

A star crept across the sky and became a plane. So few stars, you could count them if you wanted to, if you thought it was worth it. I wanted to take Sonny's hand. I wanted us to spread our wings and lift straight out into the air like hawks. My heart thudded away inside me with Sonny's awful truth. My brother had killed people. Where was I supposed to put that? Where did that fit with the Sonny I knew?

I followed Sonny back to the car, his words echoing in my mind. Why had he told me? I'd never have found out. He didn't have to tell.

Did he admit what he'd done because Lawrence hadn't? Was he saying something about Lawrence, something I needed to remember and to heed, or only something about himself? Did he tell me only because he couldn't hold it all inside himself any longer? I didn't know. I didn't even know how to ask. And anyway, I'd finally stopped expecting Sonny to answer my questions, to solve all my problems. Nobody could do that but me.

Did it take everybody fifteen years to figure out such a simple thing?

Sonny reached for the ignition. Then his hand dropped away. "I wanted to make Dad proud. Remember that? What a joke."

"Dad *was* proud of you! It's in the cookbook!"

Sonny looked at me like I'd blown my gaskets.

"It's true. It's right there, between the roast beef and the meat loaf!"

His face cleared for just a minute, the way clouds thin into nothing after a storm, leaving the sky. "I missed you, kiddo," he said.

"I'm not going to cry," I said. All I did was cry. I'd had enough of it.

"Okay," he said, but his arm went out, and I dove for him, sobbing and sobbing like the fourteen-year-old I would never be again.

We were quiet going down the mountain, but it was the good quiet, an old overcoat kind of quiet.

We passed the bowling alley, Bagget Brothers, the Esso station, and finally the Frostee. Jason stood under the neon Frostee sign, striped in blue-and-red light. Just Jason, nobody else. He was watching the street, as if he knew sooner or later we'd be coming by.

"There's Jason," I said, as if Sonny couldn't see for himself. When we came around the turnaround tree, I saw Jason saunter toward his car. He was waiting in the Deuce as we passed, and pulled out behind us. Sonny glanced in his mirror. I saw him start to grin, then check himself and go back inside, to wherever Sonny went.

"What's that fool up to?" he said. Jason was hanging almost on our bumper.

"He wants to race. I told you."

Sonny sighed like an old man, a weary old man.

The Deuce tapped the Ford's bumper. Tapped it again. Sonny's head shot out the window. "Hey!" he yelled. "What the hell are you doing?" Right in front of Saint Thomas Aquinas.

Another bump, this time a good one. Sonny yanked the wheel and we flew into the vacant lot, dust swirling, rising in choking clouds. He cut the engine and got out, slamming the door.

The Deuce came purring in through the dust. "Hey, Sonny!" Jason said. "Welcome home! Where you been keeping your bad self?" The best thing you could say about Jason was that he had real good teeth.

Sonny stood with his hands on his hips, looking down at Jason as if he didn't know him, and I guess he really didn't. Then I saw his shoulders relax. He reached for his Luckys. "Around," he said. He gave the pack a shake and offered a cig-arette to Jason.

Sonny lighted Jason's, then his own. They each took a drag and exhaled, as if that was conversation.

A piece of ash had settled on the Deuce's door. Frowning, Jason brushed it off. "So we gonna get it on, or not?"

"Race," Sonny said, as if the word came from some foreign language. "You want to race."

"That's what I said, didn't I?"

"Let's go then," Sonny said. He didn't care. It didn't mean a thing to him, you could hear it in his voice. Things were dif-ferent now. But Jason couldn't know that, how a race could be nothing.

"I'll tell the guys," Jason said, tapping the gas to let the Deuce sing that one bright note.

"No," Sonny said. "It's just us. It's got nothing to do with them."

Jason looked confused. "But—" You could see what he was thinking. Why race at all if nobody was there to cheer you on, to make you Numero Uno?

"Just us," Sonny said, sliding back into the Ford. Jason didn't move at first, then he turned the Deuce in a slow U and headed for Carne Road.

"And me," I said quickly.

"Cory—"

"Somebody's got to be a witness," I said. "Jason will say he won."

"It doesn't matter," Sonny said with a sigh, as if I'd missed something the first time.

"Please. Please just take me with you."

He gave me one long look, and then he started the engine.

22

SOMETHING EASED IN SONNY as we drove toward Carne Road. I could see it in the way he drove, three fingers at 6 o'clock. His face looked happier, lighter, and even with that hair, he looked more like the brother I knew. "Mom's doing good," he said. "She's doing real good, isn't she?" He glanced over, waiting for me to agree. But he'd caught me by surprise.

"Uh, yeah. Fine."

"And Sam. She can handle that, right? I could kick his butt, if you think—"

"No, oh no! He's a nice guy. Anyway, Mom says he doesn't ring her bells."

Sonny laughed. "That's good," he said. "I was worried about her. You know, about how she would do without Dad. But she's fine." He shook back his hair. "You, too."

I shrugged. "Sure. I mean, I guess . . ."

"The whole country's changed." He shook his head, as if he'd never understand. "Weird," he said. "It's just weird."

I didn't want him to stop talking, so I didn't say a thing.

"It's like the world went right on. Like I wasn't even in it. You know?"

I didn't. How could I?

"It's just damned hard to know where you are sometimes." His face grew dark and troubled again. Then he forced a laugh. "Hey," he said, "I'm not losing it. Don't worry."

"I know," I said. "I know you're not losing it."

He didn't mean the race.

Jason was waiting at Carne Road, leaning against the Deuce with his arms crossed. He almost pulled it off, the screw-you-and-the-horse-you-rode-in-on look, his favorite. But something gave him away. Maybe his shoulders were too high, his arms too tight, the famous grin too fixed, but he wasn't the old Jason.

Sonny pulled up beside him. "I'll take Cory to the other side," he said. Jason would have punched the gas and fishtailed, if it had been him. But Sonny took his time, like we were going on a Sunday drive. I closed my eyes, tried to keep my heart where it was. And suddenly, I wanted the kids to be there. At least Lisa. Somebody. Jason was right. Why race at all if nobody was there? But Sonny didn't even need me there.

He made a turn at the wall and stopped. The engine had a different sound now, high-pitched, impatient. I opened the door. "You gonna be all right?" Sonny said, from a long way off.

I got out, hugging myself, shivering in the heat. "Yeah."

"Back in a flash," he said.

"Let him beat you, Sonny," I said.

"Jason?"

"Yeah. Let him win."

If only I could have read the things that went through Sonny's eyes then, but I couldn't. Around us, a sea of orange trees, their leaves whispering night secrets.

"Roll up the window," Sonny said. I did what he said. "Shut the door," he said. And so I did that, too, closing Sonny behind the glass. His thumb went up and he grinned. Then he chirped the tires twice, to make me laugh, and sped off. But I didn't laugh. It was all I could do not to cry. A long time ago, it would have felt right to be there. Even with the fear, it would have been no more than a thing we did.

Climbing the water tower, I caught a splinter in my thumb. It was good, in a way. A good hurt. For a little while, I could sit on the wooden ledge, pick at my splinter, and feel sorry for myself. From not far enough away came the yipping cry of a coyote. I forgot the splinter and drew up my knees, hugging them hard.

Why was this night so different? The kids weren't here, sure, but everything else was the same: same grudge, same Jason, and me with the same deep fear that kept me from breathing right. It was Sonny who wasn't the same. He looked almost the same, he did the same things with his life, messing with cars, not much else. He smoked now, that was different. He didn't laugh much, or even smile a whole lot, that was different, too. He carried a weight inside him now that showed in the way he walked and sounded, and even stood, slouched and wary.

But it was more than all that. Sonny didn't care anymore. It hit me like a splash of ice water. Sonny didn't care. And I knew right then, when it was too late, when I couldn't do a thing, that Sonny shouldn't be racing. If you didn't care, nothing kept you from going straight through the wall.

I laid my forehead on my knees, tried to keep my stomach from coming up but it was no use. Leaning over the ledge, I threw up Mom's meat loaf. Well, threw it down, I guess. Wiping the snot and puke and tears off my face with my sleeve, I prayed, *Hail Mary, Mother of God, pray for us sinners now and at the hour of our death. Amen.* I said it like the peace chant, all jammed together, over and over. *Hail Mary, Mother of God, pray for us sinners now and at the hour of our death. Amen. Hail Mary, Mother of God, pray for us sinners now and at the hour of our death. Amen.* I'd learned something from Saint Thomas Aquinas, after all.

And then they were coming, two engines singing to each other, winding up, then shrieking above the trees like banshees. Headlights pierced the dark, four yellow dots on black. I stood up, shaking, crying, talking to myself, to Sonny, to God. Sonny wasn't going to come through this, I knew that now. It was like God had given me a preview to get me ready, to help me hold on. Sonny would lose. If you didn't care, you had to lose.

Both hands over my mouth to keep from screaming, I stood, frozen, as they came headlong down that dark tunnel of a road. The rocks were lit now, the Ford and Deuce past the halfway point. "Sonny!" I screamed then. "Sonny! Stop!" The night filled with the thrum of pounding pistons, both engines pushed to the screaming edge. The Ford leapt forward, then the Deuce, then the Ford again.

———————

All the worst things in life happen in slow motion. Why this is, I will probably never know. The best things flash by like hummingbirds too fast to catch, the worst things stretch themselves out like bad company and hang around, letting you see every piece of everything, so you can remember for the rest of your life exactly how it was.

The wall, the tower, my bare legs in cut-off jeans, my cool sandals, polished toenails, a thousand trees, two windshields, everything alive with light, moonlight, headlights, as the Ford and the Deuce came rushing toward the wall. Jason's face was pale and his narrow eyes as open as they got, fixed ahead on the rocks, fingers gripping the wheel like claws.

But Sonny? Sonny was smiling, gently smiling as if he'd remembered some sweet, nice thing. A song maybe, or a kiss. I screamed his name, crying, choking on my sobs, but of course he couldn't hear. Then the squeal of brakes, tires burning, smoking, fighting for traction, as the Ford stopped short and the Deuce fishtailed in a wide screeching arc and slammed sideways into the wall.

As if shot from a cannon, Jason's body flew out into the trees, a dead perfect dive.

I don't remember scrambling down off that water tower. But Sonny was there, I remember that. Sonny looking wild and scared and young, most of all young. We ran through the trees like kids playing hide-and-seek, only no one was laughing. "This way!" I yelled once, because somehow I knew. Or remembered that arc through the air, Jason tossed like a rag doll. The moon cast tree shadows in the spaces between, and it was hard to see. "Jason!" yelled Sonny, as if he was angry, as if Jason was breaking the rules. "Jason!"

Sonny came around one way, I came from another, and there was Jason.

He was covered with blood, so much you could hardly tell who he was, or even what he was. He was lying on his back, one arm bent under and his body twisted sideways. Sonny knelt, put his ear to Jason's mouth. "He's breathing," he said. "Stay with him." Sonny took off running through the trees.

I knelt beside Jason, afraid to do a thing. I knew, because you do, that I shouldn't move him. "Jason?"

Only the leaves spoke, in that soft way they have.

"Jason."

He opened his eyes like he was waking up from a long nap in a strange place. He lifted his head and looked all around.

"Don't move," I said. "You're hurt."

But I could see he didn't know me.

He closed his eyes again. Nothing to wipe the blood with, so I took off my T-shirt, wiped his face with that. Blood bubbled from his nose in a stream I couldn't stop. Smell of burnt rubber mingling with the sweet smell of orange blossoms. What were we doing here? No way to answer. I felt the way you feel before sleep, that swimming you do in your mind, pieces of dreams gathering, almost peaceful. I was tired like never before in my life, and guilty for wanting to sleep, to get away.

Jason groaned just once, tried to move his arm. I laid my hand on his forehead to say, *Keep still, keep still.*

We could have been there for hours, nights, no way to know. At last, a siren, thin and high, from a long way off, then closer, then here, and a wash of red light spinning, spinning away and returning, spinning away and returning. In the red light, Jason looking black, as if he'd been burned.

I heard them running through the trees, branches breaking, leaves slapping. Sonny's voice, "This way! He's over here!"

"It's okay now, Jason," I said, smoothing his forehead, smearing blood. "They're here. It's okay now. You're going to be okay now." If that counted as a lie, I didn't care.

They laid the stretcher down beside him. I felt hands under

my armpits, Sonny lifting me. "My shirt," I said. Sonny picked it up, pulled it gently over my head, a tie-dye of blood and dirt. Sonny's hands were shaking, his fingers icy cold. Jason was on the stretcher and they lifted it, four men, hurrying away through the trees to the ambulance, its light still twirling. Sonny put his arm around me, led me from that place, past Jason's Deuce, buckled like a tin toy hurled against a wall.

I huddled under Sonny's arm as he drove, my teeth chattering so hard my jaw ached.

"Breathe," Sonny said.

The emergency room was lit like a circus, which is how I guess it always is. A nurse took one look at my shirt, my blood-covered legs, and was ready to check me in. Sonny said we were there for Jason. She handed me a wet towel and said we could wait in the waiting room, which is all I remember of that.

I woke up hot and sweaty on an orange plastic couch, but I knew right where I was. "Sonny?" I stumbled outside, the smell of dried blood clinging.

Sonny was standing in the middle of the parking lot, smoking a cigarette.

He frowned. "You okay?"

"I fell asleep. Is Jason—?" I almost said "alive." I still couldn't believe it.

"He's okay," Sonny said. "He's a mess, but he's okay."

It was quiet outside, four cars in the parking lot, the moon a pinched face.

"Why didn't he stop, Sonny? Why didn't Jason stop?"

"Because I didn't," Sonny said. Tears welled up in his dark eyes. He blinked them back and looked away. I watched him take a deep drag on his cigarette, then another, saw the way he put it out between his fingers, as if he'd lost all feeling.

23

THERE WERE MORE THINGS WRONG with Jason than a regular dictionary had words for: concussion, rupture, laceration, contusions, bruises, breaks, you name it. For a week, no one but his mom and dad were allowed see him, and then only for a couple of minutes. But Sonny and I went every day anyway. We didn't even talk about when we'd go or even if we'd go. We'd have our breakfast, then we'd drive to the hospital, sit in the waiting room, and read old copies of *Life* magazine. For Sonny, it was catching up on history. I tried to find the newer stuff. *Time* for August 16, the day Jason went into the wall, had Richard Nixon and Spiro T. Agnew on the front. They looked a little shady to me, but after President Johnson showed his appendix scar to everybody in the world, well, I'd had enough of him.

Mom was full of questions. I let Sonny do the answering. It wasn't easy for him, lying to her, but he seemed to take it as his job, and so I let him. "It was bound to happen sometime,"

Mom said, shaking her head. "Racing like that on the city streets. You'd think he'd have more sense at his age."

The *Ojala Sun* had a picture of the smashed Deuce on the front page. "According to Corin Davies, who happened on the scene with her brother, Brian," the story said, "Jason had been practicing for one of his infamous New Year's Eve runs."

When Sonny's medical discharge finally came, he didn't seem to care one way or the other. Dr. Loomis said Sonny's leg would never be right. He said it in medical language, but that's what he meant.

The Ford was back in the garage. When Sonny drove, which wasn't very often, he took Dad's Dodge.

We didn't see Sheila at the hospital the whole first week. I guess she knew not to come, but it did seem strange that she waited so long. Sonny and I were sitting in the waiting room as usual when she showed up. Sonny was reading me the *Los Angeles Times* cover story. An antiwar demonstration at the Democratic Convention in Chicago had turned into a full-scale riot. I knew Lawrence would have been right there fighting in the streets, if he could have been. I wondered if they let him read the *Los Angeles Times* in jail. Maybe they just let him have the Bible. But probably, with all those fancy lawyers, he'd never gone to jail at all.

When Sheila popped her head in, Sonny did a double take. But I'd already heard about her hair, which was orange to match the bridesmaids' dresses. "Hi, Sonny!" she said, fluttering the tops of her fingers. "Hi, Cory."

"Hi, Sheila," Sonny said, his voice as flat and empty as a runway at the drags.

"Seen Jason yet?" She touched her poofed-up curls, I guess to see if they were still poofing. Her lipstick matched her hair dye so perfectly, I wondered which came first. Her eyes had the strangest way of looking like nobody was home. Still, they were the prettiest bright blue. Like an empty summer sky.

The nurse was going to let us know when we could go in, I said.

"Aw, come on," she said, jerking her orange head toward the hall. "They'll let us in. I'm his wife. Well, almost."

I looked at Sonny. Sonny shrugged and got up. He looked so worn out. I don't know if he slept or just sat on the back porch all night smoking cigarettes. All he thought about was Jason. You could tell by the way he dragged him into every conversation. *Remember when Jason . . . ? You know, Jason . . .*

We followed Sheila's skinny little butt down the hall, hanging back as she stuck her head into every room looking for Jason. He was in the very last one.

"Jason!" Sheila cried. "You poor sweetie!"

Jason was a sight. His left leg hung from a pulley thing attached to the ceiling, and his right arm lay across his chest in a fat white cast. From the neck up, except for a patch on his forehead, he was pretty much the same, which was a relief. Sonny had told me all about head wounds, how they bled and made things look worse than they sometimes were. He'd been trying to keep me from worrying.

Sheila bustled around like the wife she was practicing to be. She kissed Jason's forehead, smoothed the sheet over his chest, chirping the whole time like a redheaded woodpecker.

Jason looked lost, his grin lopsided, as if it had been cracked in the accident. He kept trying to work it, but it just wouldn't. "Hi, guys," he said. "Come on in. I don't bite." He held out his left hand for Sonny to shake. They shook like old friends, which they weren't. But there was something between them now that wasn't there before, and it was bound to stick. "Hey, Sonny," Jason said, all serious. "Gotta ask you a favor."

"You got it," Sonny said quickly. I could see how relieved he was that Jason was going to let him do something. "Name it." He'd have done anything for Jason. He'd have given him the Ford without a second thought.

"How about being my best man?"

"Oh, goodie!" Sheila said, going up on her toes, clapping her little hands.

"Uh, *sure*," Sonny said. For a second, I thought he was going to laugh. Then, because Jason looked so serious, he got serious, too, his eyebrows drawing together over those dark, troubled eyes. "Like I said, anything you want. I mean that, Jason. Anything."

207

"Hey, man," Jason said, his voice blurred around the edges, "this isn't your fault."

Sonny nodded slowly, but you could see he was hearing only the words inside himself.

"We're going to have the wedding right here!" Sheila burbled. "The whole thing, Father Julian, all the bridesmaids and groomsmen and everything! And, guess what, Jason honey? It's the greatest thing!"

Jason made a real effort to smile, but you could see how it cost him. "Yeah?"

"Daddy's giving us a new car for a wedding present! A brand-new Chevy station wagon!"

Jason's face looked almost the way it did before he went through the wall. Like his future was coming on too fast, a big surprise he should have thought a little more about. But it was too late now. Sheila was popping the Whitman's chocolates I'd laid on the nightstand. She was a skinny girl, but from the side, you could see pretty clear how the future had already started.

Mom offered to cater the reception. "A nice smoked salmon dip, I think, and a cheese plate. Pickles and olives . . ." We told her everything would have to be at the hospital. "Well, then, there needs to be enough for the doctors and nurses." She started jotting things down in her notebook. Sonny put his arm around her. She looked up, surprised. "Thanks, Mom," he said.

The day before the wedding, getting ready for my lunch

shift, I glanced out the upstairs window and there was Sonny walking past Saint Thomas Aquinas, heading home. It took him a while, because he had the limp now. It was strange to see him walking, almost as strange as seeing Lisa walking.

"Mom?" I heard him call as he came in.

"Mom's at Bayley's," I said, heading downstairs. I followed Sonny into the kitchen, steamed up and smelling of onions. Mom came pushing through the back door with her hip, arms filled with Bayley's bags. Sonny took them from her and set them on the prep table.

"Twenty-nine cents a pound for green beans! Outrageous! I got collard greens instead."

We put the groceries away. Mom tied on a clean apron. "I want you to try the soup," she said. "It's Dad's onion soup. You wouldn't think soup would be so hard to get right."

"Look, Sonny," I said. "Right here."

I flipped the cookbook open to "Meats" and pointed to the place where Dad's words were scrawled down the margin.

"Huh!" Sonny said. Just that. But I thought he lightened up a little after that. Stood a little straighter, maybe.

Mom filled three bowls and made us sit in the dining room. The soup had croutons and plenty of melted cheese. Imported, not Velveeta. "It's good, Mom," I said. "Perfect."

Sonny agreed. We didn't even have to lie. Mom was becoming this great cook.

Sonny reached into his back pocket and pulled out a folded

envelope. He put it on the table in front of Mom. "For the bills," he said. "Dad's funeral, the hospital . . ."

Mom looked at Sonny, then down at the envelope, a puzzled look on her face. She opened the envelope and took out the bills. Hundreds. They looked brand-new. "Where did you get this?"

"Sold the Ford," Sonny said.

At fourteen, I'd have gone straight through the ceiling, but now I understood.

"Oh, Sonny, you didn't have to do that. We'd have paid it all, sooner or later."

"I know," Sonny said. He cleared his throat, as if he were about to make some long speech. But all he said was, "I'm going to take off."

"Oh," Mom said, getting up, stacking the bowls. "Well, okay. Do you want a sandwich first?"

"I'm going away, Mom. I'm going away for a while." He shot a quick, worried look at me.

"I don't understand." Mom looked lost. She sat back down, as if she couldn't trust her legs to hold her up. "Where will you go?"

"Canada, maybe. North." Sonny shrugged, like it didn't much matter which direction he went in. Whatever he was looking for wasn't in some special place. It sure wasn't in Canada, which is where we should have gone to begin with. But it wouldn't have helped to point that out. It had taken me one whole year to learn when to keep my mouth shut.

"Gotta figure things out . . ."

"Oh, sweetheart," Mom said. She reached across the table and grabbed Sonny's hand so hard her knuckles turned white.

"I'll be all right," he said. "Don't worry."

"That's what you said the last time!" Mom wailed, which was when I realized I'd already cried through a stack of paper napkins.

"Well, I came home, didn't I?"

Feckless tried to scramble up into Sonny's lap, her tongue all ready to wash his face.

"Can't you figure stuff out here?" I said, but I was wasting my breath.

The wedding turned out better than you'd think. The nurses really got into the spirit of it, draping Jason's room, and even Goose's wheelchair, with white crepe paper. Paper bells hung from the pulley hook over Jason's bed. Sonny found a tuxedo jacket at the thrift shop and cut the front off so that Jason could more or less wear it. Sonny looked so handsome in a new charcoal gray suit. His dark hair was pulled back in a ponytail and so you saw his face more, how his nose wasn't perfect but that it didn't matter. It was just a part of who he was.

The room was chock-full of people by the time Sonny pushed the button on the tape player and the wedding march started up.

I peeked out the door and here came the pumpkins, Lisa,

then Melodee, then Candy, Jimbo's little sister. I waved at Lisa and she smiled, giving me a big wink. Even as a pumpkin, Lisa was gorgeous. Jimbo was her groomsman, but they had broken up. For sure this time, she said. They weren't even touching.

Sheila came next, dressed in white taffeta, a long white lace mantilla trailing the linoleum. Her smile was pure Pepsodent. Last of all came Father Julian in his white robes and golden tassels, a fat white Bible in his hands.

Jason looked at Father Julian like his fate was a firing squad, but by the end you could see he was ready enough to be a husband. He gave Sheila a big juicy kiss and everybody cheered. The honeymoon would have to come later, not that they hadn't tried everything out already.

We toasted them with champagne in paper cups. Mom passed around platters of food. Sonny and I held the cake so that Sheila and Jason could cut it together. They did the face mash with the frosting, and that was pretty much that.

I helped Mom clean up. "Ask Sonny to take this out," Mom said, handing me a bag of trash.

There were so many people in the room, I couldn't find Sonny at first. Then I did. He and Lisa had gone out into the hall. You'd have thought they were a couple, or at least real good friends, the way they were talking so quietly, Lisa glowing, the tiniest little smile on Sonny's lips. They didn't even see me. I went back and grabbed the trash myself.

The next day, we set Dad's stone, the one that Sonny had ordered a few days after he got home. It said what we'd planned all along: SPENCER EDWARD DAVIES, 1916–1967, LOVING FATHER AND HUSBAND, carved in pink marble edged in gray. Nothing fancy. Like Sonny said all along, Dad wouldn't have wanted anything fancy. Sonny set it himself, digging the hole so that the stone would lie flat and even.

It was just a marker, after all. Dad lived in our memories, in all the old stories. "Remember when Dad banged the toilet seat and said he'd shot Sam?" "Remember when Dad danced Maria off the porch?" "Remember when Dad kissed Mom right in the middle of the dining room and all the people clapped?" "Remember when he pulled the accordion straw out of his nose?" "Remember when he farted so bad we all had to run downstairs?"

At last, Sonny and Mom turned to leave. I slipped a bay leaf out of my pocket and laid it on the stone.

Mom glanced back, her eyes eagle sharp as they'd always been. "Is that a bay leaf?"

"No," I said. "It's an oak leaf."

"Oh," she said uncertainly.

That night I couldn't sleep. I knew what Sonny was up to. From the time we got home from the cemetery, he was already moving away. Turning in before either of us, he'd said good night the way you say goodbye. Mom went over and hugged him hard, her head against his chest. She knew what was happening. "Sleep well, son," she said. "I love you so much."

Sure enough, as the sky began to lighten, I heard Sonny moving quietly around his room, putting things into his backpack. I had to let him be. It was what he wanted, and I could give him that, but it was the hardest thing I'd ever done. Sonny had promised he'd write every week. It wasn't much to hold on to, but we'd hold on anyway because that's all we'd have. Mom was fine. I'd said it myself. And I was fine, too. Even the country would find peace. Now it was Sonny's turn.

I listened to his uneven footsteps going down the stairs, Feckless right behind. It took everything I had not to run after Sonny, not to grab him and say one more time how much I loved him, how I would always love him with all of my heart, no matter what he did or where he went. But that would have been for me, not for Sonny. Sonny wanted it this way.

Feckless began to whine. "Shush now," Sonny said. I heard him set his pack on the floor and he must have knelt, because what he said next got muffled in Feckless's fur.

The front door opened, then closed quietly. I jumped up and ran to the window. The first rays of morning light were creeping up over the mountains. Sonny was standing at the edge of the Avenue, wearing his fatigues, the big green Army pack on his back, and a peace sign drawn on with black ink. He surprised me when he turned and looked up, but I didn't surprise him. He knew I'd be there. He held up his hand, I held up mine. Then he turned and crossed the Avenue.

It could have been the sun, the golden light that seemed to follow him as he strode away, his hands clutching the straps of his pack. It could have been the sun, but I think it was Dad.